RAGING FIRE

BY

MARY BRANDT GOLOVERSIC

Watercolor painting on cover by James Goloversic, Sr.

ISBN: 0-7596-8305-0

This book is printed on acid free paper.

1stBooks - rev. 04/12/02

Acknowledgment

Scripture quotations are from a King James Version of the Bible printed for the Gideons by the National Bible Press in 1957.

Chapter 1

Eric was puffed out. It was a warm sunny day in Upper Michigan, even with an occasional cold east wind blowing off Lake Superior. Eric was sweating hot. He had started out before dawn to go into town. He had worn a light on his head to show the way in the dark. All went well until the sun came up a few hours later. Now his cross-country skis were sinking into the foot of new fluffy snow that was on top of the old snow. The soft snow was clumping up in the grooves in the bottoms of his skis, the ski binders were catching on the bushes as the skis sank to lower levels, and the heels of his ski boots were slipping on the smooth melting snow accumulating under his heels.

Usually Eric took his swift Polaris snowmobile into town, but today it wouldn't start. A series of snowstorms were predicted for the next few days—one storm after another—and Eric needed food, a new typewriter ribbon, and carburetor parts for his snowmobile.

Sometimes the twenty miles into town was a pure pleasure trip, but today wasn't one of those days. Eric still had six miles to go, but he was far past the seasonal part of the road. "Seasonal road" in the Upper Peninsula was fancy language for unplowed! It had been easy skiing on the snowmobile path on the unplowed road in the cooler pre-dawn hours, but breaking trail in the snow beyond the top of the snowbanks of the plowed road was difficult, especially with the hot rays of the sun melting the new snow.

Eric decided to stop alongside of the plowed road and clean the snow off his skis and ski boots. He skied on until he came to a straight level stretch of road, a relatively safe place to stop. Carefully, he went down the four-foot high snowbank sideways until he reached the plowed road surface. He stuck his ski poles in the snowbank, unsnapped the ski binders that loosened the binders. He stepped out of the binders of the right ski. Using that ski as a tool, he chipped the hardened snow off the heels of his right ski boot and off the bottom of the ski. Then he took off the other ski and repeated the process. Having accomplished this, Eric felt a lot better. He paused to take a breather before continuing on.

Then he jumped to the sound of a horn behind him. He was on the edge of the road, but cars tended to slide in the winter, even on straight stretches of road.

A new sport utility vehicle pulled up, a forest green Ford Explorer. A cheerful feminine voice called out, "Are you out for fun or skiing into town?"

Eric looked up. There was a pretty face surrounded by the fake fox fur-edged hood of a white parka.

"It's town day for me," replied Eric.

"Want a lift into town?"

"Sure. That would be great. The snow is really sticky today—not a good time to ski."

The young woman hopped out of her vehicle and walked around to the far back and opened the lift gate, so the skis and poles could be put in.

"My name is Tanya Brandt."

"I'm Eric Carlson." He loaded in the skis.

"I've heard of you. You're the writer who moved up here last fall." Tanya slammed down the lift gate, walked back to the driver's door, and got in the driver's seat, while Eric got in the passenger door. Off they went.

"You live on the seven acres out by Beaver Creek, don't you?" asked Tanya.

"Sure do."

"How do you like living out there?"

"Well, it's a quiet place to work."

"I'm going to work now."

"Where do you work?"

"At a little bookshop."

"The one downtown on the corner?"

"Yes."

"I noticed that it's called 'Job Books.' Do you specialize in business books about jobs?"

"No," Tanya cheerfully corrected with a smile. "The "Job" refers to the Job in the Bible."

"Oh," said Eric, the wheels of his brain turning fast to remember who Job was. "He's the one with all the patience."

"Yes," agreed Tanya.

"I sure could use more patience. Waiting ten years to get books published can be a bit trying. I keep writing more books as the ideas come to mind, but I haven't been able to get a publisher to even read any of the books."

"It's hard, all right," said Tanya. "Thousands of manuscripts come into the publishers every year. Some get a reading, some get a glance, and some don't get considered at all. I guess it's the same with many writers, artists, and musicians—play 'the waiting game."

"Well, if nothing happens by fall, I think I'll pack it in and go back to my regular job. I'm living in the old-fashioned way now, and that can get to be a bit rough."

With the lively conversation and the short trip by car, they were soon at the stoplight waiting to cross the highway and head downtown.

"Any special place you want to be dropped off?"

"The office supply shop would be fine."

Tanya drove there, pulled up into an empty parking place, and parked. She waited for Eric to unload his skis and poles.

"If you're in town all day, I'll be glad to give you a ride to the end of the plowed road at five."

"I appreciate the offer," said Eric, "but I want to start back early, because a storm's moving toward us."

"Well, bye for now."

"Thanks a lot for the lift."

Eric watched Tanya drive off in the Explorer and then stuck his skis and poles in the snowbank and entered the store to get his typewriter ribbon.

* * *

Eric finished his errands quickly, but, that fast, the sky had begun to turn a stormy gray. He had loaded everything into his packsack and returned to the office supply store to retrieve his skis and poles and head for home. He put the skis together, bottom to bottom, and heaved them up over his right shoulder and carried the ski poles in his left hand.

Then he headed north to his cabin. After a mile, he crossed the highway. The traffic quickly thinned out as the houses became spaced further and further apart. In the silence, Eric began to think. *Why did I open my hurting heart to a stranger, a young woman I just met?* He always kept his publishing problems to himself. In fact, he was a rather private person, except in the classroom teaching history to seventh graders.

Well, he told himself, *no time to think about that now.* He had reached the edge of town and crossed the bridge. It was time to put on his skis, climb up the snowbank to the soft snow, and begin the trek back so he could get home before the storm settled in.

* * *

When Eric arrived back at his cabin, he was hot from the exertion of rushing back. Snowflakes were beginning to swirl around his head. At least the snow hadn't been so sticky towards the end of the trip, but it was a bit icy when the wet snow froze.

Eric stuck his ski poles in the snowbank next to the snow shovel by his cabin door. Then he took off his skis and cleaned the snow off of them and stuck them in the snowbank beside the poles. The skis had to be kept outside, because, if the skis were kept in the cabin, they would be warm, and the snow would stick to them the next time he needed to use them.

Then Eric headed for the outhouse—his current bathroom. It was a small narrow hut built over a deep hole that had been dug out. There was a bench seat built over the dug hole with a hole cut into the boards, a size to fit a human's bottom. On top of this was an oval of Styrofoam with a hole cut out of its center—a warm toilet seat for a cold winter day. After relieving himself, Eric shut the door, turned the homemade wooden latch, and went back to the cabin.

Inside the cabin, it looked cozy, but the air was cool. The fire in the woodstove had burned low while he was in town.

Eric took off his mittens and rubbed his hands together to get the stiffening chill out of his bones. Then he reached for the black poker, bent down, opened the cast iron stove door, and stirred up the coals. He set the poker back down on the stone floor and added some chunks of split wood to the fire and shut the stove door.

He walked over to the dry sink and grabbed a metal bucket and a big blue and white enameled pan with a handle and went back outside. He walked down the path to the spring. He bent and filled the pan with water and dumped it into the bucket. He kept doing this until both the bucket and the pan were full, and then he carried them back to the cabin.

Eric put the water bucket under the dry sink and filled the big cast aluminum kettle with the water from the pan. He put the kettle on top of the woodstove to boil.

Already the cabin was warming up. Eric looked around. His temporary home wasn't much like his apartment near Detroit. There were no painted walls or real sink or full-size electric stove or refrigerator. No toilet or tub or TV. No furnace. No air conditioning. No Lazy Boy recliner. No near neighbors.

Still, this cabin was really more homey than his apartment. He missed his parents. His dad worked in a Ford factory. His mom contentedly stayed home to be a full-time wife and homemaker. He missed his mom's home cooking. Eating canned pork and beans could get to be a bit boring. Even so, Eric liked his current surroundings and cabin.

The property owner, who had carpentry skills, had built the cabin on a rock above a tiny waterfall. The distance the water dropped was small, but big enough to give a small, but constant, sound of falling water. It sang its bubbly song as it rushed downstream into a bigger creek and then into the Dead River Basin.

Across from the little creek, a tall cliff rose, seemingly reaching up into the sky.

The cabin was built to blend in with the environment. The man who built the cabin had cut the pine logs from his original forty acres of land. He skinned the bark off the logs and let them dry a year before building.

Concrete had been poured for the building slab and a block wall built for the back wall against the rock. Half-logs covered the cement blocks of the back wall, and the other three walls were made of full-size hand-hewn logs.

There were three small narrow windows on the creek side of the cabin. A window was on each side of the entry door; these were a little larger and square and overlooked the trail along the creek. At first Eric disliked the small windows, but, when a bear appeared one night, he was glad some of the windows were small. The bear left paw prints on the larger windows by the door. Eric kept those windows boarded over for a few weeks after several visits from the bear. He missed the natural light, but it was better to be in dimness than have a bear intrusion. At the back of the cabin, there was a larger window overlooking the swamp below; this window was out of the reach of the bear.

The floor of the cabin was in three levels, following the elevations of the rock. The wood stove was below the main floor in the right-hand corner behind the door; this part of the floor was made of stones to be fireproof. The other levels of the cabin floor were made of wide planks. The main floor was on the creek side, at the level of the entry door and extended all the way to the back window. The floor on the left side of the cabin was elevated like a platform in a church.

Up on the platform by the entry door was the sofa with a view of the cliff above the creek. In the center of this level against the half-log wall were some rough-cut shelves. Above the shelves was a board with six big pegs for hanging clothes. In the far corner of the platform floor was a homemade bed built against the half-log wall. Two logs went from the front corners of the bed to the ceiling, and wide twigs entwined between these vertical logs to decorate the bed in a naturally beautiful way.

At the foot of the bed on the level of the main floor, there was a low shallow cupboard for canned food. Beside this, in front of the big window at the end of the cabin facing the marshland, was a portable typing table, a wood chair, and an old manual typewriter. Without electricity, there was not the luxury of an electric typewriter or computer.

Near the typing area, along the wall facing the creek, there was a pine cupboard holding a two-burner camp stove and a dry sink holding the old metal dishpan on top and water bucket below. Between the sink and the woodstove, there was a small rustic homemade pine table and two chairs.

The owner of the cabin was renting the cabin, because he had moved to Florida for the winter. If he decided to stay in Florida year-round, he would sell the cabin the following autumn.

Soon the kettle began to boil. Eric got out a heavy tan mug with an owl on it, put a teabag in the mug, and filled the cup with the hot water. How Eric wanted to sit at his typewriter with a cup of tea and gaze out at the swirling snow in the swamp, but there was no time for that now. The snowmobile carburetor was a priority. A leisure cup of tea and writing would have to wait.

Eric would have to be satisfied with a quick cup of tea. He gulped it down as fast as he could. He lit the green Coleman lantern, unpacked his carburetor parts, and went out to the toolshed.

Chapter 2

Tanya paused from sorting mail and looked out at the steadily falling snow. It was only three o'clock, but the snow was building up fast. Even with a four-wheel drive vehicle, it would be wise to leave for home early. She set down the mail, went over to the door, and turned the "OPEN" sign around to "CLOSED." She turned down the thermostat for the furnace and emptied the till. She'd make her bank deposit and head out north to her house.

She slipped into her white leather Sorrel boots and her white parka. Tanya wasn't prideful about her appearance, but she knew she looked well. She had dark blue eyes, warm wide lips, and straight long blond hair. She was as graceful as a young doe. With the white parka, she would blend in with a forest of birch trees.

Tanya went out of the store, locked the door, and headed along Main Street towards the bank.

The female bank teller asked, "How's the storm coming along?"

"A few inches—so far," replied Tanya.

"The radio announcer said to expect a blizzard. Late November storms can be nasty. I'm glad I go home in an hour."

"It'll feel good to get home and stay home," said Tanya.

Tanya left the bank, walked to her Explorer, and opened the door. She got in, turned on the engine, took the combination ice scraper/snow brush, and got out to clear the windows. First, she went all the way around the vehicle and brushed off the roof, so the snow wouldn't blow on the windows as she drove. The handle of the tool was long enough to reach most of the snow. Then she went around the vehicle again, brushing snow off the windows and scraping off ice. Then she brushed the snow off her clothes and got back into the truck. She pressed the heater button and put the car in four-wheel drive. Tanya knew she probably wouldn't need to use four-wheel drive this early in a storm, but she felt more secure knowing all four wheels were engaged and ready to provide extra power when it was needed.

The six miles home were quick ones, and soon Tanya was turning left into her half-mile long driveway. She soon reached her garage. Tanya pressed the garage door remote control button, and the garage door went up. She drove into her garage, flipped the button to lower the large garage door, went out small entry door, and closed the door behind her. She walked up the road to her house that was on the crest of a hill overlooking a long valley. The visibility was rapidly decreasing in the storm, and she could not see across the valley.

As she walked up the path to her house, her outside light came on automatically. It was still daytime, but the storm made the remaining daylight so dim, that the light was activated when Tanya came in range of the light sensor. Arriving at the side door of her beautiful home, Tanya picked up the shovel she had set near the door and shoveled the snow off the doorstep. Then she unlocked the door, shook the snow off her parka, stamped the snow off her boots, and went inside.

Dusk was arriving early. Tanya flipped on the light switch. She took off her jacket and boots and put on a pair of soft deerskin moccasins. She filled the teakettle and turned on one of the electric stove burners. Time for tea and a fried egg sandwich. After she made her supper, she'd sit in her recliner and check the weather channel and then read a novel. She knew there would probably be a power outage. During almost every storm, a dead tree would blow down somewhere in the area, and wires would be downed. She had her quiet Honda generator ready to keep her furnace and water pump running. She'd be O.K.

As she settled down with her tea, sandwich, and TV weather channel, she had to wait for the local forecast to come on, and her thoughts wandered back over her day.

Tanya thought to herself, *That stranger from out north seemed to be a nice man. He was about six feet tall and well built. His hair was blond like mine, but wavy. His eyes were blue, but not as dark as mine. He seemed a gentle sort of person and kind with a warm smile*.

Tanya thought, *I'd like to get to know him better. I sell books, but I haven't met many writers. I wonder what he did before he came here. I wonder if he's married or has a girlfriend.*

Sitting up with a jolt, Tanya spilled her cup of tea on herself. *Why ever am I thinking of that? Eric's personal life is none of my business. Or is it?*

Tanya took an honest look at her line of thinking. *Eric is a man I might grow to like quite well.*

* * *

Tanya was twenty-seven, college educated, and an only child of wealthy parents, but she had met nobody to whom she felt seriously attracted. She'd dated for years and received two proposals, but no man had been able to fill the empty spot in her heart.

Her parents live twenty miles away from her in Marquette in a beautiful Victorian home on Ridge Street overlooking Lake Superior. Tanya loved them very much, and they loved her.

Tanya's paternal great-grandparents had arrived in Marquette in the 1800's, and her grandfather, a surveyor, had begun his real estate business by purchasing a good tract of land as a young man. The venture had turned into a prosperous real estate company, and Tanya's father was now worth millions. The family had a summer cottage in the Huron Mountains, and Tanya fully enjoyed her time there, but she wanted to taste independence.

Realizing their daughter needed to leave the nest, Tanya's parents hoped for a way for Tanya to taste freedom, but not be too far from home.

Then Tanya and her parents learned from area Christians at church that some people in a nearby town wanted a Christian bookstore. Tanya's parents discussed this with each other and decided to offer Tanya an opportunity to open a bookstore.

When they presented their daughter with the proposal, she was so excited, she began to jump with joy like a child. An opportunity to serve God and be on her own. What an answer to two of her prayers! She gave God a silent word of thanks. She hugged her parents.

Her father then had two other surprises. "I own a corner storefront in that city, and it was recently vacated. It would make a nice bookshop. I also have a real estate listing for a modern house on eighty acres of land. Does either one interest you?"

"Does either interest me? They both do!" shrieked Tanya. "When can we go and look at them?"

Her mother said, "How about tomorrow after church?"

"Terrific," exclaimed Tanya.

Mr. and Mrs. Brandt knew they would miss seeing Tanya on a daily basis, but they wanted what was best for their daughter.

* * *

Sunday was a beautiful fall day, a perfect time for a ride in the woods. As the Brandt family turned north off the highway to drive to the house that was for sale, Tanya was fascinated with the vivid foliage, the shining lakes and rivers, the wildness of it all. Turning into the colorful woodsy lane that led to the house, Tanya spotted an old log homestead. She asked her father to slow down, so she could look at the old house better.

"That's not the house I'm showing you," teased her father with a grin.

"I wonder who lived there," commented Tanya wistfully.

Her father replied, "I heard it was a young couple, and that the wife died in childbirth while the husband was working with a logging crew further out north."

"How sad," said Tanya's mother.

"The young husband," her father continued, "was so heartbroken that he left the area, leaving most of his belongings behind."

"Let's stop and take a peak inside," requested Tanya.

"Don't you want to see the new house first?" asked her mother.

"In just a few minutes, but I'd like to look here first."

"All right," replied her father, stopping the car.

Tanya hopped out of the car in a hurry, followed by her parents.

"Don't go inside," warned her father.

Tanya paused and looked back and asked, "Why?"

"I've been here before. The floor is rotting out."

"Well, the door is half off the hinges, so it'll be easy to see inside."

The inside of the house was dim, though. The few small windows were darkened with soot and decades of grime.

As soon as Tanya's eyes adjusted to the dimness, she saw that the homestead was almost empty. Then she spotted a cupboard in the kitchen end of the one-room cabin. It was about four feet high and had a screened door on the bottom and rows of small drawers on top. "May I have this cupboard in the kitchen of my house?" asked Tanya.

"You haven't even seen the house yet," Tanya's father reminded her. "And, if you do decide on the house, I'll hire some men to take out the cupboard safely."

"I think you take after your mother for liking antiques," said Tanya's mother with a smile, "but that one's a bit too primitive for my tastes."

"It suits me just fine," responded Tanya.

The three people went back to the car and drove on. Soon a regular garage and a large utility garage came into view. Tanya's father explained the advantage of letting the County Road Commission have access to the property. The county's truck drivers would plow the long driveway to get to their equipment stored in the garage at the end. Having plowing done was a big plus in northern winters, especially for a single woman living alone.

The house was one-story and long, set on a high spot of land and built to take full advantage of the spectacular view of the valley below. It had many large windows, and the windows pleased Tanya. She remarked, "All those windows will make it seem like the forest is inside."

"You and your trees," laughed her mother.

Mr. Brandt unlocked the door and let his wife and Tanya go ahead of him into the house. Tanya was enthusiastic and thrilled beyond measure.

They entered the kitchen, then walked through the living room and master bedroom—all with views of the valley. The bathrooms and spare bedrooms were built on the far end and faced the road. A stone fireplace was in the living room on the wall facing the road. All the appliances were modern, but the knotty pine walls, cupboards, shelves, and closets gave the house a rustic look.

Tanya looked out the large living room window and spotted a doe and two fawns down in the valley. Her parents looked at each other. They knew what Tanya's decision would be.

Teasingly, Tanya's father said to his daughter, "I suppose it'll take you a few weeks to think it over and decide."

Instantly she replied, "I know now! Yes, yes, yes!"

Tanya's mother continued teasing, "I don't suppose you'd like to furnish it with antiques, would you? Your father and I agreed to buy the furniture."

Tanya's eyes got huge. "Really?"

"Really," asserted her mother. "Would you like to start looking tomorrow?"

"Yes. As soon as the shops open."

"So much for my Monday morning sleep-in," said Tanya's mother, faking a sulky expression.

"You'll probably be ready before me, if it's antique shopping," teased Tanya right back.

"By the way," said Mr. Brandt, "whatever happened to my daughter, the business woman?"

"Oh, oh. I almost forgot. The store. Let's go and look at it now. I don't want to leave my work for God out of my plans. Let's head in." Tanya walked toward the door.

Her parents looked at her. They were truly blessed. A lovely, loving, young woman willing to serve the Lord.

* * *

The tour of the antique shops was fun and fruitful. The furniture was delivered as soon as the sale of the house was complete. Of course, the homestead kitchen cupboard had a place of honor in the modern kitchen, and its little drawers were already filled with herb teas. Two primitive chimney chairs stood on each side of the living room fireplace, and a flat-topped wood trunk set between the chairs served as a tea table. A brown wicker settee and two rockers with forest green and tan checked cushions faced the valley view. A television set stood beneath the row of windows, but it was low, so it didn't block the view.

Tanya had chosen Eastlake furniture for her bedroom, but her favorite piece was a pine pie safe with two spoon-carved doors on the front, two drawers above, and punched tin sides. It was so old that it had a small picture of a face of a Victorian lady on the top surface, probably left from the ink of a newspaper a hundred years ago. Tanya refused to wash it off. It just made the pie safe more special to her.

* * *

With guidance from the owner of the Christian bookstore in Marquette, Tanya was soon set up, stocked, and ready to open the newly painted shop. She chose to name the shop after Job in the Bible, because she always likes the heart-breaking story of Job, especially the last chapter where God restored everything to Job. She remembered the encouraging words from Job 42:10; "...and the Lord gave Job twice as much as he had before."

Tanya hadn't found romantic love yet, but she had her love of the Lord, and she was a happy young woman filled with the joy of Jesus.

Chapter 3

December arrived with another snowstorm, but then front with a high pressure moved in and all was clear. The good weather held, so Eric decided to take his monthly trip into town. His snowmobile was running again, so it would be a much easier trip than the last one was.

When Eric got to the huge park on the edge of town, he parked his snowmobile, because snowmobile use was not permitted in town, except on the east-west snowmobile trail through the center of town, and Eric had to go north-south. He put on his backpack and walked the last mile into town.

Tanya had been on Eric's mind since he met her a few weeks ago. He decided to make his first stop the bookstore. A bell over the door rang as he entered the shop. He heard her cheerful voice from the back room, "I'll be with you in a few minutes. Yell if you need me sooner."

Yes, thought Eric, *I need your company right now*. But he didn't say anything.

Eric began to browse. He was used to looking for factual history books and historical novels that aided his teaching and writing careers. Christian books were a whole new realm for him. He knew about Bibles, of course, but here were many versions of the Bible and all sorts of books. Christian history and map books, Christian devotionals and Bible study guides, and books of Christian living advice. There were Christian songbooks and tapes and CD's and videos. There were Christian greeting cards, pictures, Tshirts, and jewelry. The children's section included Christian books, games, and stickers. Eric was astounded.

"Hi," said Tanya as she came out from the back room. "We meet again. I had a big stack of boxes in the storeroom ready to topple, so I had to straighten them."

"It's nice to see you again," said Eric with a smile.

"Are you looking for anything special?" asked Tanya. She thought, *Me, I hope*.

Yes, thought Eric, *YOU!* He almost said it aloud. Instead he said, "Just a bookmark I guess. I didn't know you sold such a variety of things here."

"There are so many ways to learn more about God. With computers, there are even more new approaches to finding and understanding His original Words."

This was a bit over Eric's head, so he remained quiet. It would be better than inserting his size eleven foot in his mouth.

To fill in the awkward silence, Tanya showed Eric the display of bookmarks. Not realizing he did so, Eric frowned in confusion. Seeing this, Tanya said, "Here's the perfect one for you. It says "…with God all things are possible."" She handed him the leather bookmark with the Scripture quote of Matthew 19:26. "This includes publishing your book," she added with an encouragingly smile.

Continuing the conversation by going to a more general area of interest, Tanya asked, "Do you use a computer word processing program for your writing?"

"I did in Detroit, but my cabin doesn't have electricity, and I don't own a laptop, so I'm back to using an old

Olympia manual typewriter. It's getting harder to find the older style typewriter ribbons, erasers, and erasable paper."

"I suppose so," said Tanya considering. "I never thought about that before. You're on the beginning part of the books—writing them. I'm just on the finishing end—selling the books."

"That's really important," praised Eric. "If nobody sold our books, there wouldn't be much sense in writing."

"I guess we're a team then," joked Tanya. Then she blushed. *Maybe he would consider the comments as being forward.*

Eric thought, *A young woman who still blushes. That's rare*. The thought prodded him on, and, like a teenage boy, he blurted out, "Would you like to go for lunch today?"

"Well, I usually eat lunch in the store, because I run it alone, but going out for lunch would be a real treat. I'll make a sign saying, 'Be back after lunch.'" She took a few moments to make the sign and tape it on the door.

Wow, thought Eric. *Progress. A lunch date.*

Maybe he cares after all, thought Tanya. *Maybe I do, too*.

She slipped on her boots and jacket. Eric held open the door for her to go out first and then he went out. She locked the door.

"Where to?" asked Tanya.

"You decide," replied Eric. "I'm new around here, so I don't know much about the restaurants."

"Do you like cudighi?"

"What's that?"

"It looks like a big hamburger, but it's made with spicy Italian sausage. The owner of the Italian restaurant makes it himself."

"Sounds good to me," consented Eric.

They crossed the street and went around the corner to a tiny restaurant and deli. They went inside and found a table by the window.

"I'm a real people-watcher," confessed Tanya.

"Me, too," said Eric. "I excuse the nosey habit by saying it gives me more material for writing."

"I can't use that excuse," said Tanya with a grin.

Eric chuckled.

"What did you do in Detroit before writing full-time?" Tanya asked with real interest in her eyes.

"I taught seventh grade history."

"Did you enjoy teaching?"

"Teaching active young teenagers is challenging, especially trying to make old facts come alive, but I did enjoy it."

"Are you going back to teaching?"

"I have a one year leave of absence, so I have to make a decision by this summer. I can rent the cabin awhile—at least until the owner decides if he wants to spend his summers up here or live in Florida full-time. He's going to live in Florida this summer for the first time in the hot season and then decide whether or not he will sell the cabin."

"How are you surviving winter in the wilderness?"

"I stocked up on canned goods last fall, but the menu isn't too varied when you eat canned goods most of the time—canned spaghetti, ravioli, stew, corned beef hash, pork and beans. Canned fruit and vegetables. I could cook up dehydrated eggs and pasta and potatoes, but I seldom take the time to cook a real meal. I miss my bananas, salads, real milk, and eggs—they don't survive the cold, bumpy, snowmobile ride real well. The eggs get scrambled in the carton. My apples are beginning to wither. At least I can bring home apples, bread, bacon, ground beef, and chicken today."

Eric realized the conversation was all about him and full of his complaints about canned food, so he turned the talk back to Tanya by asking, "Where do you live? What do you eat?"

Tanya briefly described her house in the woods, purposely leaving out the details of luxury, so he wouldn't feel so bad about his situation. Instead, she briefly described her house and then described in detail the old homestead cabin on her land. She told Eric about her menu. "You know, I have a stove and refrigerator, but I shortcut on cooking. When I get home from work, I'm satisfied with a simple meal and a good book. I sure look forward to the potluck suppers at church." She glanced at her watch. "I've been gone for over an hour! I have to get back to the store. How long will you be in town?"

"Quite a few hours. I have to do some history research at the library for my novel and then a little shopping."

"The high school drama club is putting on Dickens', *A Christmas Carol*, tonight at seven. Would you like to go? We could grab a hamburger to hold us over."

"Sure. When should I pick you up?"

"Five-thirty should be fine. The high school is only a few blocks from here."

They got up to leave. Eric helped Tanya on with her jacket and then slipped back into the upper part of his snowmobile suit.

"I might look a bit off going to a play in a snowmobile suit."

"It's winter. In the UP, nobody will notice," said Tanya, and then added, "Well, maybe a few will, but it doesn't matter to me. Does it matter to you?" she asked, looking up sincerely into his eyes.

"Not at all," said Eric with a comical smile. "When in the Upper Peninsula, do as the Yoopers do, right?"

"You know that I'm a Yooper—U.P.-er. Do you know *you* are a Troll?"

"I've heard that I am. Because I live below the Mackinac Bridge, like the troll under the bridge in the kiddy story, *Three Billy Goat's Gruff*."

Tanya linked her arm through Eric's. "Come on, Troll. Walk the Yooper back to her store."

"Certainly," said Eric, bowing and donning a gallant expression. Laughing, the two went out the door of the restaurant.

As they parted at the door of the store, Eric thought, *I really like her*. Tanya gazed up at him, and he thought he saw a glimpse of a look of love in her eyes.

Chapter 4

Tanya spent Christmas in Marquette with her family, and Eric spent his day alone at his cabin. He'd received a Christmas package from his parents and was enjoying the homemade frosted sugar cookies and wearing the hand-knit scarf and tassel hat. He brought a few sprigs of cedar inside to decorate the tiny kitchen table. The cedar fragrance filled the room. He had some candles for emergencies, and he lit one on Christmas Eve.

As he opened the woodstove to add more wood, he saw the blaze and thought of Tanya and the fire of love burning in his heart.

Tanya was thinking the same thoughts as she gazed into the flames in her parents' fireplace. The ornate white marble mantle was adorned with real holly leaves and berries, brass angels, and white candles in tall crystal candlesticks. A ten-foot tree stood in a corner decorated with white balls and gold bows.

The room was filled with people from her father's office, people from the neighborhood, and from the golf club. It was the Brandts' annual Christmas Eve open house. Most of the people were over forty. The few younger adults were full of chatter about fashions, real estate prices, and New Year's Eve parties.

Tanya pushed herself to be sociable. She usually spontaneously enjoyed parties, but tonight she was thinking about how much she missed Eric.

* * *

January was a month of storms, but, even with bad weather, Eric increased his trips into town from once a month to once a week. He asked Tanya out for lunch each time he was in town, and she accepted each time. Their relationship was growing closer and closer. Now they held hands, and, when they had a few private minutes at the store, they kissed. Tanya hadn't asked him over to her house, and Eric hadn't asked her to his cabin.

One Sunday afternoon in February, Tanya impulsively decided to drive to the end of the plowed road that ran by her house and then ski the rest of the way to Eric's cabin. There had been no recent snowstorms, so she knew she could follow a snowmobile trail. She knew where the cabin was located. She also knew Eric was likely to be at his cabin, because he didn't come into town on Sundays when the office supplies store and snowmobile dealership were closed.

Tanya had spent a wonderful three hours in church that morning—a Bible study and worship service plus a potluck fellowship lunch. She felt relaxed and ready to hit the trail, so she gathered together her ski equipment, loaded it into her Explorer, and drove north. When she reached the end of the plowed road, she parked the Explorer, unloaded her ski equipment, put on her skis, and began to ski the rest of the way.

By three o'clock, she smelled wood smoke, and soon she saw smoke from the chimney of Eric's cabin. She herringboned her skis up the steep trail to his cabin—ski tips outward—and snowplowed down the other side—ski tips inward—and rounded the bend. First she saw Eric's snowmobile, toolshed, and outhouse. Around the next bend, she saw the cabin sitting peacefully in the sparkling snow.

Tanya skied up to the door, stuck her poles in the snowbank, removed her skis and cleaned the snow off them, and stuck them in the snowbank next to Eric's skis. All was quiet, except for a chickadee, crying his "chick-a-dee-dee-dee-dee-dee" call. At least chickadees stayed all winter. Robins—the state birds—deserted Michigan and migrated to warmer places in the winter.

Timidly, Tanya knocked on the door. No reply. She knocked louder. No reply. She was determined not to ski back without seeing Eric. She opened the door and peeked in. There he sat with his back to her, rapidly typing away, lost in the world of fiction.

Tanya called to him, "Hi, Eric!"

He turned around so fast that he almost tipped over his chair. "Tanya!"

"It was such a nice day, I thought I'd ski out to visit."

"Are you all alone?"

"Of course," she replied pertly. "Aren't you going to ask me in?"

"Sure, sure." Eric sheepishly stood up and walked toward her, as she stomped the snow off her boots before entering.

"Let me hang up your jacket." Eric helped her off with her jacket and hung it over a chair near the stove. "Are your feet wet?"

"No, but the tops of my ski socks are."

"Take them off. I'll hang them to dry."

Tanya sat down on a chair near the fire to take off her ski boots and socks, but before she could bend over, Eric was down on his knees untying the laces.

"I can do that myself," asserted Tanya.

"I know you can, but I want to do this."

Tanya sat back contentedly. How good it felt to have Eric be so considerate.

"I'll lend you a pair of my socks and moccasins. They're way too big for you, but the floor is cold."

"I have extra socks in my backpack."

"But yours are cold. Please use mine."

While Eric searched for the socks and slippers, Tanya gazed around the room, memorizing every detail of Eric's home. Weeks ago, she realized she loved Eric, and now she'd be able to visualize him at work while they were apart.

Eric knelt and put on the thick socks and soft slippers.

"It feels good to wiggle my toes," sighed Tanya.

"Would you like a cup of tea? Are you hungry?"

"I ate a lot of lunch at church, but I would like a cup of tea."

Before long, Tanya and Eric were sitting at the tiny rustic table drinking their black Lipton tea. They talked about the weather for awhile to break the ice of their first occasion of being completely alone. Tanya wanted to say how much she liked the twig work on the foot of the bed, but it seemed too intimate to mention his bed. Instead she asked Eric how his writing was coming along.

"Would you like to see any of the manuscripts? I have them all here, so I can do revisions when the ideas come to me. The latest novel isn't finished yet."

Tanya looked them over. "I see they're all historical novels. May I read the one about World War II?"

Eric had never lent out a manuscript, but for Tanya he'd make an exception. "Sure. You can take it with you today. It's quite bulky, but it'll fit in your backpack."

"Speaking of backpack, I'd better head back. It's already turning to dusk."

As she reached for her socks, Eric gently put his hand on her wrist to stop her. "You are not skiing in alone."

"I've skied alone at night before, and there's a full moon tonight. I have a headlight in my backpack, too."

"Other snowmobilers use part of the trail, and they might not see a skier or they might be drunk and speeding." Eric paused. *Should I tell her the whole truth? Yes, I will.* "Even if there were no danger, I'd want to go with you. I enjoy being with you." His heart skipped a beat. *Have I overstepped the boundary*?

Tanya looked up, and this time there was a lasting look of love in her eyes, not a fleeting glance. She replied shyly, "I'd be happier to be with you longer, too."

A bit embarrassed, Eric stood up and said, "In that case, I formally ask you to dine with me."

"I accept," said Tanya with a giggle. Tanya thought, *I'm glad the emotional moment has passed. Eric's isolated cabin is too secluded a spot to let my heart run wild.*

"Could I interest Mademoiselle with canned beef hash, delicately fried in a black cast iron skillet, and topped with catsup?"

"What a superb suggestion. Certainly." Tanya paused and switched from formality to informality. "May I help?"

"You, Tanya, are the honored guest. Sit back, relax, and watch me work."

Within half an hour, Eric had the table set, the hash fried, apple cider heated, and paper towels folded for napkins. The catsup bottle served as the centerpiece for the tiny table. Eric sat down, and they both began to eat.

"This tastes really good," complimented Tanya.

"It looks like canned dog food, but has a great taste," said Eric.

"I wonder what canned dog food tastes like," pondered Tanya.

"I hope I never have to find out," laughed Eric.

By the time supper was finished and they had talked a bit more, Tanya said it must be about eight o'clock. "I'd better get going. I have to open the store at nine in the morning."

"I guess I'd better not try to detain you any longer," Eric said, faking sadness, hanging his head. Eric admitted to himself, *I am covering up my true feelings. I want to hold her tight and kiss her over and over again.*

They quickly put on their outer clothes and loaded the manuscript into the backpack. Eric had a snowmobile sled, so he put Tanya's skis and poles in that.

They got on the snowmobile—Eric in the front, and Tanya in the back. He turned the key, warmed up the engine, and then revved it a bit. When the engine sounded ready, he yelled to Tanya, "Hold on tightly to my waist."

"O. K.," she shouted above the engine noise.

"Ready," yelled Eric.

"Ready," confirmed Tanya.

The Polaris skimmed down the trail with ease. The moon brightly lit the area beyond the snowmobile headlights. All too soon they arrived at the Ford Explorer.

Tanya got off the snowmobile, stretched, and walked to the SUV. She got in, put the key in the ignition, turned the key, and the engine purred. She got back out. Eric had already loaded the ski equipment into the back of the truck.

"I'll let the engine warm up a few minutes," said Tanya.

Eric could no longer restrain himself. He pulled Tanya into his arms and said over and over, "I love you. I love you. I love you."

Tanya's answer was immediate. "I love you, too. I love you so much."

It was a cold night, and the young couple had many layers of thick winter clothing between them, but the fire of their love seemed to pass from one heart to the other. They rocked in each other's arms, back and forth, again and again, until Eric fell backwards into the snowbank still holding Tanya.

Suddenly the words of love turned into peals of laughter, as they slid down the snowbank and ended up landing on the snow-packed road.

Tanya grew silent first. "I guess the engine must be warm by now." Then, mischievously she added, "I won't need to turn on the heater. I'm plenty warm." Before Eric could comment on that remark, she jumped up and didn't even pause to brush off the snow. She opened the truck door, hopped in, and slammed the door shut. Off she drove with a final "Toot, toot" of her horn.

Eric had finally gotten to his feet and stood there stunned. *What a woman*, he thought, shaking his head in happy amazement.

Chapter 5

February vanished quickly with Eric's more and more frequent trips into town. He was head over skis in love.

Tanya never again skied to Eric's cabin and still hadn't invited him to her home. Eric didn't invite himself to her house or ask to be invited. They both knew that being together alone would cause too much temptation.

Tanya was in love as much as Eric was, but suddenly she became aware that she had spiritual reservations about the romantic situation. She had been a Christian for many years and knew how important it was for two people in love to be together also in their faith in God. Yet, she had allowed the romance to escalate to high levels and still knew nothing about where Eric stood with Christ. As easy as it was to talk with Eric, he seemed to go silent when the talk turned to religion. Tanya wondered why. She didn't know that Eric did not know how to reply, because he did not know what Tanya was talking about when she talked about Bible verses and mentioned Christ as her Savior, God her Father, and the Holy Spirit her Guide. Eric felt ignorant and was ashamed to ask her to help him understand.

His parents went to church on Christmas and owned a Bible, but the Bible was as new as the day it had been given to them. Eric knew the history of Christianity, because he taught it in his history classes, but he had only facts, no personal understanding and little knowledge of the Scriptures.

Easter was near the end of March, and Tanya decided to break the ice on the pond of religion by asking Eric to go to their church's special sunrise service and give him an invitation to the church Easter Sunday breakfast, Bible study, and worship service.

It was a lot to ask, but Tanya needed to know whether or not she and Eric were united spiritually. If not, she would have to break their wonderful romantic relationship. She prayed and prayed for courage, and God gave it to her.

Either way, she would have to dampen down her physical desire to be dangerously near Eric. She remembered the Bible's advice against burning with lust. The fires of her heart needed to be banked until she got married, if she got married.

* * *

As usual, Eric visited town that week and stopped at the bookshop as soon as he got into town. "Hi," he said brightly. "How's life treating you?"

"Pretty good, at least until I have to do income taxes. April 15 is getting closer. Speaking of dates, Easter is in March this year. Our church has a hike up Sugarloaf Mountain north of Marquette for a sunrise service on Easter." Tanya's words kept tumbling out faster and faster, like water over the waterfalls in springtime flooding at Eric's cabin. "We meet at the foot of the mountain at 6:30, climb to the top, have a short service, climb back down, go to the church, eat breakfast, change our clothes, go to Bible study, and then the regular worship service." *There. The words were said*, Tanya thought as she silently encouraged herself. Hesitantly she added aloud, "Want to come with me?"

Eric was stunned into silence. *Did this mean three church meetings in one morning?* He only went to church once a year, and last Christmas he had even missed his once-a-year attendance of a service.

Tanya, too, was silent.

Suddenly Eric became aware that Tanya was waiting, afraid of his response. *Well*, he thought, *I can handle three services with Tanya at my side. Besides, one service is in the woods! I won't count that one.*

His face broke into a smile. He said, "Sure. Count me in." He could hear Tanya's audible sigh of relief and see the tenseness drain out of her body.

"You're on," she challenged. "I'll pick you up at the end of the plowed road at 5:00 to save time. I know the road is just breaking up beyond there. Can you get up that early?" she challenged.

"I'll be there, even if I have to buy an extra alarm clock to make sure I wake up."

"I'll keep you to your word," warned Tanya.

"Not to change the subject, but are you hungry? It's lunchtime," said Eric.

"Already? I was working so hard putting out Easter items that I didn't realize it was that late. Now that you mention it, I'm hungry! Let's go."

The conversation was back to a simple subject: food.

* * *

Easter morning arrived dry and clear. Eric wanted to drive to meet Tanya, but the road was really muddy from his cabin to the sandy jack pine plains. He didn't want to tear up the road or get stuck or lose a muffler with his low-clearance two-wheel drive car, so he took his mountain bike. With his bike, he could walk around the mud holes and remains of snowdrifts. He wore his jeans and hiking boots and put his dress clothes in the bike bag.

The light on his bike gave just enough illumination to see the two tracks of the road. His bike wheel took a few sharp unexpected turns in the mud and snow, but Eric kept his balance.

Tanya was waiting at the end of the plowed road. There was still a bank of snow at the end of the road where the snowplow had turned around all winter. It would be a few weeks before Eric could drive into town.

Tanya hopped down from her sport utility vehicle and opened the lift gate in the far back for Eric to load his bike. He first emptied the clothes out of the bike bag and then loaded the bike into the Explorer. Eric offered to drive, and Tanya accepted.

By the time they drove into town, went east on the highway and north on the road toward Big Bay, it was 6:30 when they got to the base of Sugarloaf Mountain.

Several cars were already in the parking lot. Tanya and Eric got out, each with a flashlight.

There was a wide trail up the mountain with wood steps in the steepest parts. They scared up a deer that ran across the trail. When they were partway up the trail, the sky started to lighten, and, in the distance, they saw the charred trunks of trees burned in a forest fire the fall before.

"Think of how terrible that fire must have been," said Tanya. "The animals must have been so afraid, seeing the flames and feeling the intense heat."

"And the trees," added Eric. "It must have taken them decades to grow to that height, and now all that's left are tall black skeletons of the trees."

"I hope the animals escaped the fire," said Tanya.

"I do, too," agreed Eric.

By the time they reached the top, the fog was lifting above Lake Superior, and the sun was rising. People were wandering around looking at the magnificent views of the lake beyond the treetops and examining the monument constructed of stones. Some of the people heard Tanya and Eric approach, and they turned and greeted the couple. A few said, "Happy Easter," "Welcome to the top."

Tanya and Eric walked over to the edge. The drop down was steep and rocky. They saw the morning sun shimmering on the surface of Lake Superior far below.

Soon one of the men walked over to the flat grassy spot in the center of the summit and asked everyone to find places to sit. Tanya and Eric found a flat rock to share for a chair. The service began with the group singing "The Old Rugged Cross." Most of the people knew the words to the song, but Eric didn't recognize the song; yet its words made the message of Easter more meaningful. The sermon was short, and the story of the crucifixion and resurrection of Christ seemed to come alive, being on the summit of Sugarloaf Mountain at sunrise. *The setting,* thought Eric, *reminds me of how it must have been on the hill of Calvary with Christ on the cross; and the sunrise and stone monument remind me of the empty tomb on the morning of the first Easter.* The service closed with a prayer by the group leader and the group singing of the song, "Christ Arose." Eric could visualize Christ rising to the clear blue sky he saw above him.

A reminder of breakfast was announced, and everyone got up—stretching, brushing earth off their jeans, picking up their supplies. The youth ran on ahead. Tanya and Eric lingered at the end of the group, and, when the crowd dispersed, and Tanya and Eric got past the steep steps and on the path, the young couple held their gloved hands. The temperature was rising fast, and simultaneously they withdrew their hands, removed their gloves and joined hands again. It was a good thing they were holding hands, because Tanya slipped on a rock, and Eric caught her before she fell. They had a quick hug, a peck of a kiss, and then Tanya laughed and said, "We'd better hurry or the breakfast food would all be gone."

* * *

They drove back to Marquette and on westward to their town and to Tanya's church located in some woods at the western end of town. The parking lot was about half-full. Eric parked. They got their dress clothes out of the back seat and took them in with them.

When Tanya and Eric got inside the church foyer, they set their spare clothes on the hat shelf. Eric helped Tanya out of her jacket and hung it up and then took off his jacket and hung it next to Tanya's. They could smell pancakes and bacon as they walked through the double doors into the fellowship hall.

Most of the tables were filled with people, and nobody was in the buffet line or behind the counter, so Tanya and Eric began to serve themselves. One of the ladies came forward and offered to serve them, but Tanya laughed and said, "We slowpokes can take care of ourselves. Enjoy your breakfast before it goes cold."

Tanya took a plateful of food, a teabag, and a cup of hot water, and Eric did, too. Some people beckoned to them that there were two empty places at their table, and soon the young couple was seated.

Tanya put her egg between her two pancakes and topped it all with maple syrup. Eric had never made a pancake sandwich, but Tanya's looked good, so he fixed his food the same way.

Talk at the table was fast, free, and noisy. Those who hadn't gone on the hike wanted to hear the details of the hike. You could tell who had been on the hike and who had not by their clothing.

After breakfast Tanya and Eric went into the bathrooms to change. Being the last to eat breakfast, the two bathrooms were almost empty, so they didn't have to wait for stalls to empty. They met in the hall. Tanya looked Eric over with a smile. "Is this how you look in 'city clothes?'" she teased.

He replied, with a lopsided grin," "The woodsman put on his town look."

Eric brought their hiking clothes to the car and returned to the church to join Tanya. They went into the sanctuary for the adult Bible study.

The teacher was an interesting person, a Finnish person with a lot of Finn jokes, but a lot of serious Bible wisdom, too. He made down-to-earth applications of the Scriptures to life in the Upper Peninsula of Michigan. Eric was surprised at how he could relate to the study and understand it. For weeks he had been afraid he'd feel out of place in the church, but he felt at home instead.

In the fifteen minutes between the Bible study and church service, some men invited Eric to join them in the kitchen for coffee and doughnuts. Eric looked at Tanya questioningly, but she nodded "yes," saying she needed to practice a song with the ladies' group.

The men asked Eric where he lived, and, when they heard it was out at Beaver Creek, they were full of questions about the current condition of the roads and asked if Eric had a four-wheel drive and how he had survived the winter at camp.

In a few minutes, Tanya joined Eric in the kitchen, grabbed half a doughnut and a sip of Eric's coffee, and then they went into the sanctuary for the Easter morning service.

* * *

The service was much like the Christmas services Eric had attended at assorted churches when he was a child. There were hymns, announcements, prayer, and the taking of the offering. A group of women sang—the group Tanya was in. There was a Scripture reading with everyone reading directly from the Bible, their own or one from the pew. A man sang a solo about Jerusalem. There was another hymn, and then the pastor began to speak. Eric listened for awhile, and then his mind began to wander to the novel he was writing. Then some of the pastor's words caused him to tune in again.

"As I climbed the trail up Sugarloaf Mountain this morning, I saw the bare black trunks of trees burned in the forest fire last fall. They reminded me of the fires of hell where unsaved sinners suffer forever. As Revelation 20:15 says, 'And whosoever was not found written in the book of life was cast into the lake of fire.'

"Nobody is perfect, so we all deserve the punishment of the everlasting raging fires of hell, flames that no fireman can put out.

"However, we can have hope. Jesus came to earth to die on the cross to pay for our sins, so we won't go to hell and be engulfed eternally by flames.

"Jesus is like a Search and Rescue team leader. In Luke 19:10, we read, 'For the Son of man is come to seek and to save that which was lost.' Jesus is looking for each of us, so we will accept Him as payment for our sins. II Peter 3:9 tells us that 'The Lord is…not willing that any should perish, but that all should come to repentance.' Jesus doesn't want even one of us to be unsaved. As He, Himself, said in Luke 15:4, 'What man of you, having an hundred sheep, if he lose one of them, doth not leave the ninety and nine in the wilderness, and go after that which is lost, until he find it?'

"Here in the U. P., we have lots of wilderness—forests, rocky bluffs, and wide plains, lakes and rivers. Search and Rescue teams have formed, and these men and women search for lost hunters and fishermen, snowmobilers and hikers and campers.

"Though not all of us are lost in the woods, we are all lost in sin and headed for hell. Isaiah 53:6 says, 'All we like sheep have gone astray; we have turned every one to his own way; and the Lord hath laid on him the iniquity of us all.' The last half of that verse tells us that God put the sins of all of us on Christ on the cross.

"The payment for sin is spending our life after death in hell. However, Jesus paid for our sins by dying on the cross. Thankfully, He rose again and still lives, which is why we are gathered here today—to celebrate His resurrection.

"God offers us a Gift this Easter. It is not Easter candy or Easter eggs or Easter lilies. It is what is most precious to Him, His Son, Jesus, to pay for our sins so we do not have to spend eternity in hell, but in heaven with our heavenly Father. Jesus is a Gift, as Ephesians 2:8-9 makes clear. 'For by grace are ye saved through faith; and that not of yourselves: it is the gift of God: Not of works, lest any man should boast.'

"If you have not yet accepted this Gift, we hope you will do this today, because nobody knows what danger tomorrow will bring, maybe even death. That is why the Bible warns us in the last half of verse two in II Corinthians, chapter 6, '…behold, now is the accepted time; behold, now is the day of salvation…'

"Jesus is searching for you today. Do you want Him to rescue you from paying for your sins in a horrible place called hell, a place much worse than any forest fire?

"If you would like to accept Jesus today, please come forward now as the organist plays, 'Jesus Paid It All.' Everyone bow your head, except those who want to come up here to pray."

The organist played the song through twice, and then the pastor said, "Let's all stand up and sing, 'Christ the

Lord Is Risen Today.' If anyone would like to talk to me about accepting Christ, please tell me after church."

After the last verse of the joyful song, the pastor gave a closing prayer and went to the back of the church to stand by the sanctuary entry door to greet people. Eric took his time leaving the pew and ended up the last in line to shake hands with the pastor. As Eric shook hands, he asked the pastor if he could speak with him.

"Sure, come into my office."

Tanya turned around to look for Eric, and he told her that he would be back right after he talked to the pastor.

The two men entered the quiet office. The pastor shut the door and motioned for Eric to sit on the sofa. The pastor sat beside him and asked, "How can I help you?"

"Today, what you said in the sermon hit my heart hard, Pastor. I know now that I want Jesus."

"Do you have any questions about what I covered in my message about salvation?"

"No, Pastor. It made sense, and I believe what the Bible says."

"Would you like to pray with me now?"

"Yes," replied Eric with hope in his heart.

"Do you want to do the praying or would you like me to lead?"

"I'd prefer to have you pray."

"Then please repeat each part of this prayer after me."

The pastor went on to pray, with Eric repeating a sentence every time the pastor paused. "Dear God, I realize I am a sinner…I am sorry I hurt You with my sin…I believe Jesus was crucified for my sins…was buried, and rose again…I accept Jesus in payment for my sins…and for everlasting life with God…Thank You for this Gift…Please help me to be the person You want me to be…in Jesus' Name, amen."

Eric had tears in his eyes as the prayer finished.

The pastor said to Eric, "Remember today's date, the beginning of your new life as a Christian, as a child of God. What a wonderful Easter this is for you."

"Yes, it is, Pastor—thanks to you."

"No, the thanks and glory all go to God."

"You're right," agreed Eric.

"Well, I'm sure Tanya is waiting for you. If I can be of any help to you any time, just let me know."

"Thank you, Pastor. I appreciate your offer."

The two men stood, shook hands, and went back to the foyer.

Tanya knew what had happened as soon as she saw the joy of Jesus on Eric's face.

The two young people put on their winter jackets, the ones they had used for the hike, and left the church.

Eric said, "Let's walk around town a bit and enjoy the sunshine."

He was quiet at first, and Tanya let him be with his thoughts, though she was eager to learn the details of what had happened.

After walking a few blocks, Eric turned onto the relative privacy of a side street and burst out, "I accepted Jesus."

“I’m so glad,” exclaimed Tanya with high spirits. “I’ve been praying and praying we’d become united spiritually through Jesus.”

“You know,” said Eric, “I never realized what Christianity was all about until the pastor compared it to a Search and Rescue mission. That made lots of sense, and then it all fell into place with the Bible quotes.”

“I’m so happy for you, Eric,” said Tanya, squeezing his hand tightly.

They walked some more, and then Tanya asked, “Are you hungry? I know of a good restaurant in Ishpeming that serves turkey dinners.”

“Yes, I am hungry,” answered Eric. “I was so excited about my decision that I forgot about food. Now I know how hungry I am. I feel like I could eat a whole turkey.”

“The portions served are big, but not quite that big,” teased Tanya. And off they went for Easter dinner.

* * *

As they were preparing to leave town, Tanya said, “I know I might not see you for a few weeks. I want to see you, but I have to warn you that you’ll probably be stranded for a few weeks soon. It’s the in-between season—in between ski poles and fishing poles. We often have a late March storm, and then spring break-up begins, and the roads are sometimes impassable. You might do well to stock up on anything you might need.”

“Do you mind if we stop at the grocery store?”

“Not at all,” said Tanya.

Eric bought toilet paper and typing paper and flashlight batteries, some powdered milk and teabags, bread and butter, ground beef and spaghetti—not a lot of supplies, but a lot to take on his bike. He used a restroom and changed back into his jeans and boots and then drove back to the end of the plowed road.

After his bike and supplies were unloaded, he turned to face Tanya.

"It's been a wonderful day, Tanya. One of the best in my life," Eric said seriously.

"Yes, it has," agreed Tanya.

Eric took her in his arms, gently kissed her, and gave her a big bear hug. Then he quickly turned, got on his bike, and rode off, turning back to wave goodbye.

Tanya stood and waved until he was out of sight, and then she got back in her car.

I think I know why he left in a hurry, thought Tanya. *He probably had to leave me before he lost his head to the fire of the need for physical love that might rage within him. I know how he might feel, because my feelings for him are racing my heart as fast as a fox can run.*

Waiting for spring break-up to pass would be a long wait for both of them.

Chapter 6

Just as Tanya had forecast, the last storm of March arrived. The wind howled toward Eric's cabin from the open plains on both ends of the creek valley and came to a crashing halt at the cabin, shaking the cabin on its sturdy foundation. The wind shrieked and howled down the tunnel between the cliff and the cabin for an entire night. By morning, the snow had drifted two feet in front of the cabin door. Eric was thankful he had stocked the supplies he needed in town and brought in plenty of firewood and spring water. He was warm and safe in the cabin and spent two solid days working on his novel.

When the storm ended and the sun came out again, it was so hot that the snow began to melt as quickly as the storm had brought it.

The tiny waterfall on the creek below Eric's cabin began to gush. At the spring where Eric got his drinking water, the water came rushing and tumbling down the hill forming new gullies in the earth. Spring break-up had begun. Thankfully, Eric's cabin was high up on a rock safe from any rising water.

Eric enjoyed watching spring emerge, and every hot dry day would bring him closer to the day the road to town would be passable, and he would see Tanya again.

One day he woke up to noises down the creek from him. He quickly dressed and went out and began to walk down the trail along the creek, but the water had flooded the lower part of the trail.

Eric ran back to his cabin and out his driveway to the gravel road to take the long route to the creek. He ran, because he thought he sensed an urgency in the noises he heard down the creek.

Reaching the top of the road down to the creek, Eric saw that the creek had become a noisy torrent of trouble. He ran down to the water and saw a truck a few feet downstream from the submerged road. Someone was standing in the back of the pickup desperately waving his arms to Eric.

Thinking fast, Eric grabbed a long, thin, windfallen tree and ran towards the truck. The man on the truck yelled, "Don't go in the water. It's deep and the current is fast."

Eric shouted, "Grab your end of this tree and hold on tight. Jump down, and I'll pull this end to get you to shore."

The man took off his heavy boots and jacket to lighten his weight and set them down, grabbed the pole, and jumped in the creek.

Eric pulled with all his might, and, within moments, the man was safely on shore.

Just then, the current caught the truck and pulled it several hundred feet downstream. The boots and jacket flew out of the truck on impact and soon were sucked out of sight by the strong current.

"Thank God you came along when you did," said the man. "Every spring it's hard to drive through the water to my camp on the other side, but it's never been like this."

Eric took him back to his cabin and lent him some clothes and boots, so the man could walk back to the main road or any occupied camp along the way and get help to pull his truck out of the water. A wrecker couldn't get through yet. Eric's two-wheel drive car would be of no help in the situation; in fact, Eric could not get his car out of his driveway yet.

* * *

The spring break-up continued for several weeks, speeded up by unseasonably-warm temperatures and a few rain showers. Eric missed Tanya, so it had been a bit rough waiting for the roads to be usable but, with his work, the days crept by for Eric. He wondered if Tanya was missing him as much as he missed her.

Finally the day arrived when Eric could drive into town—the first time since November. He'd be dressed in town clothes this time, not a snowmobile suit.

The roads were passable and dry enough that the car wouldn't tear ruts in the road. The heavy logging trucks had to wait longer to use the roads; weight restrictions hadn't been lifted yet.

There were still areas of deep snow in the shady woods, but these patches of snow became smaller as Eric drove closer to town. It was amazing the snow level differences in going just a few miles further south. By the time Eric got into town, he felt as though he had driven into the real spring season.

Of course, Job Books was the first stop for Eric. The shop door was propped open with a rock, and a news report on the radio greeted him first. Then he saw Tanya's warm smile, the best greeting of all.

"Hi," said Eric with a smile.

"Welcome back to town," teased Tanya.

"How have you been?" asked Eric.

"Busy with new books coming in and gifts for June weddings and graduations," replied Tanya. *Missing you*, thought Tanya in her heart. Then she wondered, *Was it forward of me to mention June weddings?* She hadn't said it as a hint for Eric. "Have you been busy, too?" she asked.

"I got a lot of writing done when I was grounded in the north woods," answered Eric. *I really thought about you a lot*, Eric acknowledged silently.

There was a strained silence. They were a bit shy with each other after their forced separation.

Then a lively Christian song came on the radio. "What station is that?" queried Eric.

"Our local Christian radio station, WHWL. The call letters mean, 'Witnessing His Wonderful Love,'" answered Tanya.

"I'll have to check it out on my battery radio. I see it's an FM station. I hope it'll come in out at my cabin."

"There are a lot of translator sites, so the broadcasting area covers a large territory. Even some spots in Canada receive the signal."

"By the way, Tanya," said Eric, "I'd like to start coming in to town on Sundays and go to church with you."

"I'd like that a lot," responded Tanya. *Oh, oh,* thought Tanya, *if he picks me up for church, he will learn about the wealth in my family's background. Well, I should have told him, anyway—long before now. I know the Bible says in Ephesians 4:15 to be "...speaking the truth in love..." I have to live by my beliefs, not cover up the truth. I'll tell*

Eric all about my parents and grandparents next Sunday after church.

There was a silence again, except for the music. Eric began to wonder, *Was I being pushy, asking Tanya to church?* He didn't know how much Tanya wanted to go to church with him; he didn't know her thoughts on mistakenly keeping her house a secret from him.

Tanya broke into the silent gap and asked, "Do you have a Bible, Eric?"

"No," said Eric.

"I'd like to give you one, if you'd like to have one to read."

"Sure."

"Want to pick one out? They're on the shelves over there," pointed Tanya.

Eric walked over to the shelves. "Those are all Bibles!" he remarked in amazement. "I think you'll have to choose for me."

"That's what I'm here for," smiled Tanya. She walked over to the shelves, glanced at the assortment of Bibles, made a decision, and handed the Bible to Eric.

"Thanks a lot, Tanya. I'll treasure it."

Just then a customer walked in and asked where the get well cards were located. Tanya turned to help her.

Eric touched Tanya's arm tenderly to detain her for a moment. "What time for lunch?" he whispered.

"Eleven-thirty," she said in a whisper.

Eric quickly left the shop to do his errands.

* * *

Eric returned at the agreed-on time. Tanya was in the midst of helping a man choose a birthday gift for his wife, so Eric browsed. He enjoyed checking out the many things on display, and the waiting time passed quickly. It was good to learn more about what Tanya did for a living. Eric hoped Tanya's shop was showing a good profit, so she wouldn't have to skimp on basic living needs. She seemed to be doing all right with a new four-wheel drive vehicle. He hadn't seen her home yet, but he assumed it was a nice comfortable little place.

Finally the husband agreed with one of Tanya's gift suggestions, the sale was completed, the item gift-wrapped, and Tanya shut the door and turned the door sign around to read "CLOSED."

"Where would you like to eat?" asked Eric. "What kind of food do you feel in the mood for?"

Eric thought, *I feel in the mood to kiss you.* He said, "Anything sounds good after eating out of cans all winter."

"Today's pasty day at one of the restaurants. Have you tried a pasty yet?"

"Do you mean a pastry like apple turnovers?"

"No, a pasty isn't a sweet. It's a whole meal baked in a crust—beef, potatoes, rutabagas, and onions. As you probably know, we have iron mines here. The Cornish miners who came here from England used to have their wives bake them pasties for their lunch pails, so they could eat a hot meal when they worked in the underground mines."

"Well, if the pasties are good enough for the miners, they're good enough for me. I could use a homemade meal after a winter of bachelor meals from cans," laughed Eric. Then he stopped laughing. He reflected on his words. *Maybe I shouldn't have brought up my dissatisfaction with bachelorhood. I want to push or pressure Tanya into thinking of marriage. I do hope she'd be interested, though.*

Tanya and Eric left the bookshop and went over to the most popular restaurant in town where the townspeople tended to congregate. On the right side, the wall was lined with booths and tables, and there were white birch trees painted on a background of blue sky and white clouds. Painted chickadees, blue jays, and woodpeckers perched on the painted branches.

On the back wall, there was a collection of fishing rods and reels, fishing tackle, and old wicker creels.

The men who came alone congregated at the coffee counter, and, on the wall behind the counter, there were deer antlers, mounted trout and pike, and two big paintings of a moose and bear.

Being in the restaurant was the next-best thing to being in the north woods.

It wasn't quite noon, so Tanya and Eric were able to find an empty booth by the large many-paned windows.

The shyness of the young couple began to disappear, and soon they were talking about the local wildlife.

"I saw a black bear cross the road out your way last summer," remarked Tanya. "It must have weighed at least four hundred pounds."

"I saw some huge moose prints along the road below my cabin. I'm not so sure I'd like to meet up with the owner of those prints," commented Eric.

"They're huge critters, all right. I haven't seen them here, but I have seen them in Ontario, Canada. If you hit one with your car, the moose's legs break, and the moose slides up the car hood, through the windshield, and often the collision results in the driver losing his head, actually losing his head—decapitation, to be exact. A car accident with a bull moose is worst of all—they can be well over six feet tall, and their antlers can have more than thirty points on them."

"What a terrible way to die! I'm glad I haven't seen a moose on the road—or in the woods. I thought it would be great to observe one, but I don't think so now—even at a distance. I might not live to write the story of the experience!"

"Have you heard a partridge fly up in the woods yet?"

Eric shook his head.

"No? It's a loud sound, and, if you don't know is just a bird, it can be scary to flush one."

The pasties arrived. Eric looked at his pasty and sniffed the tantalizing aroma drifting up to his nose. "Ah, yes, I know I'm going to like it. What a meal!" exclaimed Eric.

"It sure doesn't come out of a can like your cabin menu," teased Tanya.

Their light conversation continued on until Tanya realized it was after one o'clock. She quickly gathered up her belongings, saying, "I'd better get back to work. Will you walk me back to the store? I'd like to return your manuscript."

"I was planning to walk you back, anyway."

When they were outside the restaurant, Tanya said, "I thought your novel was terrific. You really made the World War II era come alive for me."

"Did you really like it?" asked Eric with concern in his eyes.

"Yes, I did. And I consider myself to be a fairly good judge of the quality and appeal of a book, being experienced in the book business. Have you sent any samples of it to a publisher?"

"I sent in samples of other books I wrote, but I received only dozens of rejects and got discouraged and didn't even try to send in this one."

"Will you try again with this book, Eric?"

"Since you think it's worth a try, I will. Your honest comments are a real encouragement for me, Tanya. I've had other people say I'm a good writer, but they weren't in the book business, so I didn't know if the comments were exaggerated praise or actual facts. I'm glad you took the time to read the manuscript."

"It was a pleasure! I enjoyed the book so much. I'm glad you honored me with the privilege of reading it. It's the first book manuscript I've ever read. It was exciting to read the book in its original form."

"It wasn't quite the original. You should have seen the handwritten manuscript—full of add-ins, arrows, crossed-out lines, and corrections," Eric said with a remembering laugh.

"That would be fun to see," said Tanya.

"It wouldn't be fun to decipher," said Eric. Then he added, "I think I'll go over to the office supplies shop and make a copy of the first chapter and outline now, and then look up another publisher in the *Writers' Market* at the library. Thanks for giving me a push to a publisher."

"I'm glad to be able to help you," said Tanya seriously.

"When will I see you again?" asked Eric.

"Soon, I hope," answered Tanya, finally getting the courage to express her feelings honestly.

Encouraged by Tanya's honesty, Eric confirmed, "Soon. Gone are my monthly trips into town. With you here, I'll be in every week—or oftener," he added with a good-natured grin.

Another customer came in. Behind a tall bookcase, Eric grabbed Tanya's hands and held them tightly in his hands for a moment. He whispered, "See you soon," and then quickly released her hands, so she could tend to the customer.

As he walked down the sidewalk, there was a bounce in his steps and he was whistling. Eric was happy. Eric was in love—without a doubt.

Chapter 7

The path of love seldom runs smoothly. The root across the path of the love of Tanya and Eric came in the form of one of Eric's neighbors.

Now that the roads were open, the camp owners started to return to their seasonal camps in the area of Eric's cabin. These people did not call their houses in the woods by the name of cabins or summer cottages. They were simply called "camps," whether elaborate or plain, modern or rustic.

Eric got to meet some of his camp neighbors when he went out for walks. Just a few days after his last trip into town, a neighboring camper struck up a personal conversation with Eric.

"I saw you in the restaurant with the bookstore lady," he said. "Did you know she's from Marquette?"

"Yes," replied Eric, feeling a little uncomfortable that the conversation was about such a personal matter.

"Her family is rolling in money. Her grandfather made money in real estate—knew when to buy and sell. Her father has the same knack for wheeling and dealing."

Now Eric was more uncomfortable than before. Tanya came from a well-to-do family.

The camp neighbor went on. "Heard her father set her up with the shop. He owns about every building on that block in town. Bought her a big house on a couple of forties out north, too. But I suppose you've seen that."

Eric had heard enough—too much. "Have to head back to my cabin. Left some soup on the table with the door open. Don't want a bear to get a whiff of the broth."

"That's for sure," said Eric's neighbor with a hearty laugh. "The bears are hungry right now. A bear would like the soup, but you wouldn't like the damage he'd do to your camp. See you around."

"Sure," said Eric as he hurried off. He almost ran back to his camp, and then sat down at his tiny kitchen table. He had lost his appetite for his soup.

Eric realized, *Tanya grew up with all the money. And I served her corned beef hash,* Eric remembered with dismay.

I love her so much, thought Eric. *I can't ruin her life chaining her to a poor unpublished writer. Even if I went back to my teaching job, I couldn't expect her to live in my small apartment in Detroit. It wouldn't be fair to her.*

Eric put his head down on the little homemade table, and, for the first time in his adult life, he cried.

* * *

Eric didn't go into town that week or the next week. He finally ran low on typing paper and toilet paper and knew he had to go in to shop, but he dreaded the trip in—the trip he had looked forward to with the enthusiasm of a flaming love.

He didn't go to the bookshop. He went to the office supplies store and then to the grocery store, hoping he wouldn't see Tanya, but there she was, by the paper towels, as beautiful as ever, but with dark circles under her eyes and sad look. She didn't see him. He quickly grabbed some toilet paper and turned to leave in a hurry, but she spotted him.

"Eric," she said with joy in her voice. "I'm so glad you're O. K. I was worried you were hurt or sick." *Or avoiding me*, she added silently.

"I've been busy writing," Eric said as an excuse. "In fact, I'm on my way back out to my cabin now."

"Already?" blurted out Tanya, not stopping to think.

Eric hesitated and thought to himself, *No, I can't stay and see her. If I truly love her, I won't allow her to be a poor unimportant person like I am.* "Yes," said Eric, putting a distant tone in his usually warm voice. "I have lots of work to do. Goodbye." He pushed his grocery cart past her and headed for the checkout counter without a backward glance.

Tanya stood frozen in place, stunned. Eventually, she regained some of her customary composure and left the store with her paper towels and food items still in the vacated grocery cart. As caring a person as she usually was, she didn't even stop to consider the clerk who would have to return the grocery items back to the shelves.

She headed back towards her bookshop, but by-passed it and went directly to her sport utility vehicle. She got in the SUV, started the engine, and aimed her car toward home. She didn't remember driving home, but arrived there safely. She turned off the engine, got out, slammed the car door, and ran into her house—sobbing all the way, and collapsed on her bed.

Tanya was heartbroken by Eric's treatment of her. Things had seemed to be going so well, and then she didn't see him for weeks after he had promised to return to town soon. Tanya had invented all sorts of sensible reasons for his absence, all the while hoping it wasn't a planned absence.

After Tanya cried a flood of tears, she finally wore out and began to think again. She wondered, *Was Eric's prayer of salvation sincere?* She wondered, *Did he pray the prayer just to please me, and now is he tired of trying to pretend he's a Christian? Is he a Christian, but sliding back? Does he have a special girl back in Detroit? Did I do something to displease him? Did I say something that hurt him? Or... Or... Or...* Hundreds of possible reasons popped into Tanya's mind until, completely exhausted, she fell into a deep sleep, sprawled across the bed still dressed in her clothes and shoes.

Chapter 8

April showers arrived, and the tears of Tanya almost drowned out the fire of her love for Eric. Meanwhile, Eric was trying to force himself to put out the fire of his love for Tanya. Their emotions still smoldered, like the embers in a fire, waiting for wood to be added for the fire to burst back into a blaze.

Rain pelted on Eric's metal roof and hit the windows of his cabin and blended with the clicking of Eric's typewriter keys; the gray sky duplicated his dismal mood.

At the same time, rain dripped from the eaves of Tanya's shop and house, adding to the depressed feeling that clouded over her days and nights.

* * *

By the end of April, the spring flowers popped their heads through the fallen leaves of the last autumn. Tanya walked her land. Delicate white Dutchman's-breeches with their pairs of petals waved in the soft spring breeze, but Tanya didn't wave. The white three-petaled trilliums nodded their heads in the gentle wind, but Tanya didn't nod back. Green Jack-in-the-pulpits hid in the crevices of the rock bluff near Tanya's home. Ever since she was a child, every spring Tanya would squeeze the green and purple-striped body of Jack-in-the-pulpit to have him squeak out his sermon, but not this year. Ferns bent their faces into pools of reflecting water, but Tanya saw none of the reflections. The yellow dog's-tooth-violets she usually picked for bouquets for the kitchen table remained beneath the maple trees. The long-stemmed blue violets and yellow cowslips in the marshland were unseen by Tanya. She noticed none of the dainty white-and-pink striped flowers of the spring-beauty. Her tears watered God's garden of spring flowers and continued long after the April flowers had ceased.

Eric had to walk the rock path from his cabin to the spring for drinking water every day. Along the way, were vines of trailing arbutus with their fragrant pink and white blossoms, but Eric didn't bend to smell them. The red of the wintergreen berries with their leathery shiny green leaves were easy to spot and someone had told Eric that the berries were edible and had a fresh taste, but Eric didn't notice them and didn't feel like eating a treat if he had seen them. He didn't hear the chirp of the returned robins. He no longer leaned over the porch rail of the cabin to listen to the song of the little waterfall, music orchestrated by God. There was no song of spring in Eric's heart, only the emptiness of loneliness. At night he had only the mournful hours of the coyotes and wolves to keep him company.

* * *

Since forcing the separation between Tanya and him, Eric had poured his pent-up pain and energy into a ruthless writing spree that spurred him on to finish the novel on which he had been working all winter.

He thought that perhaps Tanya might be working hard, too, and that thought helped him feel closer to Tanya. It let him fool himself into imagining the separation was a planned absence for work, not a final parting of ways.

He hoped and prayed Tanya wasn't feeling isolated like he was, that she would have the comfort of being among family and friends and customers and church members. Perhaps singing at church would help her heal and feel happy again. Eric tried not to think about the alternative—Tanya feeling as isolated and as sad as he did. He wanted Tanya to be happy without any hurt.

Little did Eric realize how lonely Tanya truly felt, even among friends, with family, and in a crowd. Her soft heart was breaking into tiny pieces, like bits of charred wood dropping off a burning log.

* * *

By mid-May, Eric finished the novel, but faced a writer's block with no new ideas entering his mind. He went back to revising and proofreading his manuscripts. He figured he would return to the Detroit area and teach again, but he put off writing the letter informing the school of his final decision.

Since learning about Tanya's wealthy family and high social standing, the only bit of happiness Eric had was receiving a letter from the publishing company. The editor praised Eric's chapter and outline of the World War II novel and requested a copy of the full manuscript. Though Eric was pleased with this progress, it didn't mean as much to him as it would have if he could have shared the good news with Tanya. He wrote to his parents about his progress, but his heart wasn't in the mood to celebrate.

Eric had a lot of time on his hands now that he wasn't writing anything new. One day he looked at the burgundy leather bookmark he had bought the first day in Tanya's bookshop. It quoted Matthew 19:26: "...with God all things are possible." Eric thought, *Maybe, with God's help, I can heal the hole in my heart.* He began to read the Bible Tanya had given him. He prayed more. He tuned his radio to the Christian radio station.

* * *

Hot weather arrived in June, but the fires of love in the hearths of the hearts of Tanya and Eric continued to slowly smolder, getting cooler as the length of the shadow of loneliness grew.

Eric received word that his manuscript was accepted for publishing, and he received an advance for the book, a substantial amount of money that would replenish his rapidly decreasing bank account.

When Eric received the check, he dared hope that he might return to Tanya, and he thought, *Maybe someday I will be "good enough" for Tanya.* But then he realized that the printing of a book does not guarantee that the published books will be bought by readers. And the success of one book doesn't guarantee that the rest of the author's manuscripts will be successful. Eric knew he was a long ways from being a financial success for Tanya.

* * *

June turned into July, and, on the Fourth of July, Eric sat alone at his little bonfire. He thought, *How big the fire of my love was in the cold of last winter and how low the fire of my love is on this hot summer night.* He didn't realize how much he was hurting Tanya. He still thought he was protecting her from losing her wealthy way of life and slipping down to a low rung on the social scale.

Tanya spent the holiday at her parents' summer cottage in the Huron Mountains. She hiked to a high point of the mountain range and stood alone, watching the fiery sun set with vividly orange reflections on Lake Superior. Like Eric, she thought of the highs and lows of their love for each other. *How high the fire of his love was for me at the mountaintop Easter sunrise service—not far from where I now stand, and how low the fire of his love seems to be now.* She didn't know that Eric loved her enough to protect her in the only way he knew how—sacrificing his relationship with her. Walking and working had not taken away her hurting, but as least the actions filled up some of her lonely daytime hours. The hours between dusk and daylight were hardest.

* * *

Late one evening in mid-July, Eric turned on his radio that was already tuned to the Christian station. A man was speaking about prejudice.

"This may come as a surprise to you, but most of us—maybe all of us—are prejudiced in some way. God knows this. Long ago in I Samuel 16:7, God said, '…man looketh on the outward appearance, but the Lord looketh on the heart.' God told us what to do about prejudice. He told us not to prejudge others. In chapter two of Romans, verse one, warns us about prejudging people. 'Therefore thou art inexcusable, O man, whosoever thou art that judges: for wherein thou judgest another, thou condemnest thyself; for thou that judgest doest the same things.'

"We shouldn't think too highly of ourselves or others. We also should not think too lowly of others or ourselves. We shouldn't compare ourselves with other things. I Corinthians 10:12, tells us that, '…they measuring themselves by themselves, and comparing themselves among themselves, are not wise.'

"Because God created us, we are all important to Him. If we have accepted Christ as our Savior, God has a special purpose for us—the doing of good works for Him. 'For we are his workmanship, created in Christ Jesus unto good works…' Quote from Ephesians 2:10.

"God tells us in Psalm 118:8, that we need to trust in Him, not people. 'It is better to trust in the Lord than to put confidence in man.' Philippians 1:6 gives more about this. 'Being confident of this very thing, that he which hath begun a good work in you will perform it until the day of Jesus Christ…'

"Remember what Romans 14:13 commands us, 'Let us not therefore judge one another any more…' We all need to stop judging others and stop judging ourselves and let God be the judge of all, because, as Psalm 58:11 says, '…he is a God that judgeth in the earth.' Psalm 67:3-4 adds, '…O God…thou shalt judge the people righteously.' Only God can judge others, because only God knows what is in their hearts.

"I'm going to close with this blessing of Paul's from Romans 15:5. 'Now the God of patience and consolation grant you to be likeminded one toward another according to Christ Jesus…'"

Suddenly, Eric was aware of his wrong way of thinking in regard to Tanya and some other people. *I'm prejudiced against the rich and assumed they would regard me as worthless*. He also realized, *I have misjudged myself to be unworthy. In the eyes of God, I am valuable, whether a famous author or not.* He thought, *I've assumed that Tanya, being from a wealthy family, would react against my place in society. Instead of honestly talking to her about how I really feel, I've concealed my true feelings from her; I've taken away her right to hear the truth. Instead of asking her about what she thinks in her heart, I've made false assumptions. I've taken away her right to form her own opinion and then make her own decisions.*

Eric determined, *I'll go into town tomorrow and talk things out with her. I know Tanya loves me. Why did I ever let social class lines come between us?*

But that trip into town did not happen. That night, Eric's plans for a trip into town were changed when some careless drinkers left their bonfire burning in the woods when they went back to town. The fire spread to the plains of blueberry bushes a few miles south of Eric's cabin, and quickly moved across the logging cutout area.

Soon the fire spread from the plains into a stand of jack pine trees, and there the fire began crowning—jumping from treetop to treetop, spreading the fire faster and faster.

The fire raged all night and all the early hours of the morning. Before sunrise, the fire had come closer to Beaver Creek and Eric.

Chapter 9

Early in the morning, Eric heard vehicles. The unexpected sound of engines woke him up. He wondered what was happening. Then he smelled smoke.

Search and Rescue people were going camp to camp telling the people about the fire and requesting them to take their most valuable possessions, a change of clothes, a pillow and blanket, and evacuate to Marquette. Eric asked the workers about Tanya's area, and they assured him that her area was safe, so far, that the fire was many miles away and the wind in a direction away from her home.

The decision of what to take was simple for Eric with his sparsely furnished cabin. He took his manuscripts and letters, his Bible and a few other books, his battery radio and typewriter.

He headed out to Red Road. He yearned to turn left toward Tanya's, but he knew the road was closed to everything except the firefighting equipment, so he turned right and joined the stream of cars heading east toward Lake Superior.

* * *

Tanya heard the sirens and the engines of the heavy vehicles heading north all night. Tanya's first thought was of Eric. She turned on the radio for information and heard about the fire quite a few miles north of her home, out towards Eric's. No details were given, but an announcement was made that all unauthorized vehicles were to keep off the road going north. She desperately wanted to get to him, but could not. All she could do was pray.

In the morning, Tanya saw smoke to the north. She prayed a quick prayer for the safety of Eric and all people and animals that might be affected by the fire. She quickly dressed and drove out to the main road and tried to go to find out if Eric was safe, but the road was still closed to anything except emergency vehicles going north and inbound traffic going south.

Tanya turned on the TV for the morning news and saw evacuees arriving at the Superior Dome, the indoor football stadium of Northern Michigan University in Marquette. She grabbed a snack and a small can of orange juice and headed out to her Explorer. She drove to Marquette. Along the way, she thought about Eric. *Maybe he no longer loves me, but I love him with all my heart, and I won't rest until I know he is safe*.

Parking near the Dome was restricted, so Tanya parked as near as she could and walked the last half-mile.

Nobody but the evacuees was allowed inside the Dome, but there was a list of evacuees posted near the entry. Those evacuees on the list were registered and safe. Tanya scanned the list fearfully and then saw Eric's name and whispered a prayer of thanksgiving to God.

The Salvation Army had already set up its emergency canteen. Grocery stores and restaurants were sending in food. Shopping centers and local stores were donating blankets. Some campers had no town house, only their camp, so they had no place to go. Many of the evacuees were Michigan "snowbirds" who went South in the winter and lived at their camps in the summer, and these people also had nowhere to go. For some, like Eric, their camp was the only home in the area.

It was a dry sunny day, and Tanya sat on the lawn of the Superior Dome. She recalled the Bible verses in Psalm 29:7-8 about God's power over fires and everything on earth. "The voice of the Lord divideth the flames of fire. The voice of the Lord shaketh the wilderness…" She remembered the words of Psalm 86:7; "in the day of my trouble I will call upon thee: for thou wilt answer me." Tanya calmly prayed for the safety of the campers, firefighters, Search and Rescue teams, and forest creatures.

After she prayed, she looked at the entrance to the Dome and spotted Eric. He had come outside and was pacing around and around the sidewalk near the entry. Tanya jumped up and ran toward him. Eric saw her and ran toward her. They rushed into each other's arms, laughing and crying at the same time. They rocked back and forth a few moments with a hug of relief. Then they separated and went to Tanya's spot on the lawn and sat down and talked.

Eric told her the whole truth about the reason for the separation. "It was not meant to be a rejection, but my way of providing protection for you. Then I heard the Christian radio program on prejudice and that showed me how wrong my decision was. I was planning to go into town and tell you this morning, but then there was the fire. I figured you might be looking for me at the Dome, and I didn't want to miss you, so I stayed here.

Tanya cried tears of relief, knowing Eric's love for her was still strong.

Eric asked, "Will you forgive me, Tanya?"

"There is nothing to forgive. It was an honest mistake. You meant no wrong." She paused a moment. Then she admitted, "I know I wasn't completely honest with you. I covered up the truth about my family's wealth and my expensive home. I thought I was protecting you from comparing your primitive cabin with my elaborate house. Will you forgive me, Eric?" she asked with pleading in her big blue eyes.

"I know you meant no wrong, Tanya. We both made stupid mistakes, but they are all straightened out now."

"Thanks for being so understanding, Eric."

"I like you more and more the better I get to know you," said Eric with emphasis. He took a little extra air into his lungs and asked, "I love you so much, Tanya. Will you marry me?"

"Yes, yes, yes," said Tanya leaning over to kiss Eric. The kiss was a warm one, a kiss that showed the rekindling of the embers of the fire of their love.

They drew apart as some children went scampering by, followed by a tired-looking mother who was evacuated without the help of her husband who was out-of-town on a construction job.

After the family group had passed by, Eric had a sober serious look on his face. "Let's get married next month," he suggested. "We've wasted too much time already."

"I agree," said Tanya happily. "I can hardly wait." She was ready to give him another hug, but then she saw more people walking across the lawn. "Have you ever been to Presque Isle, Eric?" she asked.

Eric shook his head, "No."

Tanya went on, "It's near here and a beautiful peaceful place turned into a city park. Would you like to go there and take a walk?"

"Sounds like a good idea."

Tanya and Eric collected his few belongings from the Dome, and they went over to the park in his car. The island wasn't really an island, but attached to the mainland by a small stretch of land. It was just as beautiful as Tanya had said it was. Eric drove around the "Island" as people called it, and, then at the bottom of a steep hill, Tanya told Eric to take a sharp right turn. The road led down a short hill to a small parking lot. There were no other cars in the parking lot, probably because it was a weekday.

When they got out of the car, Tanya took Eric down to the little rocky cove first and showed him the large crevice in a rock that she liked to go into as a child. Then they walked back up the pebbly slope, across the parking lot, and over to a footpath leading to the Black Rocks above the cove.

The happy couple chose a warm rock with a pool of water collected in the hollow of a rock nearby. They sat down to watch the waves and silently held hands.

"I've been thinking," Eric said. "I've grown to like this area over the past year. It's a beautiful place with wonderful people and lots of wild woodland. Would you like to stay here or live near Detroit? I have a job waiting for me there and the sublet on my apartment is almost expired, so the lease on my apartment is due to revert back to me. I have no reason to stay there, except to be near my parents. They enjoy my visits, but are content with each other, and I know they would be happy for me to be married, too. What do you want to do?"

"Since it's all right with you, I'd like to stay. I already own my house here, so we wouldn't have rent or house payments. I'd like to keep my store. Our town needs a Christian bookstore. If you want me to be home more, I could hire a part-time clerk or even a manager, if you want a full-time homemaker."

"I wouldn't want you to give up your shop, Tanya."

"That's good, Eric, because I would not want an argument already," teased Tanya. The lightheartedness of their relationship was beginning to be restored.

Eric remained serious. "I'd like to write for another year, but I also would like to substitute teach this year. By the end of the year, I would have a clearer outlook on my writing career and be able to decide whether to keep writing full-time or look for a permanent teaching position in this area."

"That sounds sensible to me," said Tanya.

"Speaking of writing, in all the excitement, I forgot to tell you. My World War II novel was accepted by a publisher. I carried through on your suggestion to submit it. I've already received partial payment, and I'll be receiving royalties from the sales of the books."

"How wonderful! Congratulations." Tanya gave Eric an honorary hug and kiss.

After a few moments, Tanya said, "You haven't met my parents yet. Would you like to go over to their place now?"

"Yes, I would," said Eric with firmness. "Since we already decided to get married, I think maybe I should backtrack a bit and ask your parents' permission to marry you."

"I'm glad you want to do that, Eric. It'll mean a lot to them."

"You'll be able to meet my parents, soon, too. They are coming up here for a north woods vacation."

"I want to meet them. I've been wondering if I would."

"They'll love you. I know already."

"I'm glad."

They sat a few moments more, and then Tanya said, "I'm hungry. Do you want to try a sausaccine sandwich at a little shop in Marquette? It's something like cudighi."

Tanya and Eric decided to have lunch, wander around Marquette for a bit, and then go to her parent's home. They stood up and stretched and each of them rubbed their own bottoms. The Black Rocks were hard seats.

* * *

After a quiet afternoon, they returned to the Dome area. Tanya picked up her SUV and led the way to her parents' home. She pulled up at a stately old home situated on a bluff above Lake Superior. Eric pulled up right behind her. They both got out of their vehicles.

"It's sure a beautiful place," observed Eric. He was impressed with the splendor of the house. He thought of his parents' modest house in Detroit, but now he knew that the size of a house didn't matter. The people in any house were what made it a real home. He no longer felt belittled by large houses and big bank accounts. God's Word had shown him what was important. The fire evacuation to the Dome had shown him how quickly people can become materialistically equal; the campers with magnificent summer places and those like Eric had become equals at the Dome overnight. Tanya's unconditional love had been a constant encouragement to him. Through God, Eric felt confident to meet Tanya's parents.

"It's around half past five, so both of my parents should be home. I hope dinner is ready, and they have a big meal. I'm starved."

"Guess we can't live on love after all," teased Eric.

Tanya laughed, and they linked elbows and walked around to the back door. Tanya opened the door a bit, poked her head inside the kitchen, and yelled, "Anybody home? It's me, and I have a friend with me."

Tanya's mother came out into the kitchen, followed by Tanya's father, still dressed in his business suit.

"Welcome," said Mrs. Brandt to Eric.

Mr. Brandt came forward and extended his hand to give Eric a handshake.

"Mom, dad," said Tanya in a sort of shy way, "I'd like you to meet Eric Carlson. Awhile back, I told you I was dating him."

"We're happy to meet you," said Mrs. Brandt. She managed to conceal her surprise. *Yes*, Tanya's mother remembered, *Tanya had said she'd dated Eric, but she also mentioned that she hadn't seen him in many months. She had been so happy when Eric had accepted Christ on Easter*. But shortly after that, Mrs. Brandt had seen the sadness appear in her daughter's eyes. Months later, Tanya had casually mentioned that she hadn't seen him in many months. Mrs. Brandt concluded, *Something must have happened to turn matters around again.*

"Good to have another man in the house," said Mr. Brandt in a jovial tone. "I feel a tad outnumbered at times with two women."

The four of them laughed.

"Have you eaten yet?" asked Mrs. Brandt.

"Not since lunch, said Tanya, "and I'm hungry as a black bear with no blueberries," she added with a grin.

"We heard about the fire," said her father. "I called your house and store, Tanya, and there was no answer. Has the fire directly affected either of you?"

"My house is safe. Eric, will you tell the story of what happened at your camp while we eat? I'd like to check the six-o'clock TV news for an update on the fire first," said Tanya.

"There's a beef roast in the oven. I'll just turn off the stove, so we can check the news before we eat."

The four gathered in the family room, and Mr. Brandt turned on the TV. The fire report was the first of the local news. There were shots of the evacuees at the dome and assurance that all campers were probably notified by the Search and Rescue crews. There were clips of the raging fire. Then the fire map appeared on the screen, and the newscaster continued reporting on the fire, showing clips of the former raging fire and helicopters dropping water, and firemen overturning soil.

"The fire is now ninety percent contained, and, if the wind lets up, there should be no new outbreaks of fire. The rough, rocky, rugged terrain has made firefighting difficult, but the firefighters in the air have overcome that problem. The helicopters have scooped up containers of water from Silver Lake and dropped them on the parts of the fire high up in the ridges. The fire crews are now overturning soil to put out smoldering areas below the ridges. The fire was put to a halt in the plains a mile northwest of Beaver Creek junction, but the campers in that area cannot return yet because of hotspots."

Tanya exclaimed, "Praise God! Your camp is safe, Eric."

Eric said, "I'm so relieved."

The weatherman came on next. He said that earlier in the day there had been a possibility that the wind would switch to a southerly direction and put the camps and homes in the Dead River area in danger. But the wind direction had remained stable, and the wind speed was now slowly decreasing, good news for the firefighters and camp owners. So far, Tanya's area hadn't had to be evacuated.

The next news clip was a surprise. It showed the inside of Tanya's church, and the congregation was praying for safety in the fire situation and giving thanks that nobody had been hurt. The television announcer added that the church ladies had quickly baked cookies and bars for the firefighters and many church members had opened their homes to anyone who needed a place to sleep.

Then the sports report came on. The timer went on the stove. "Dinner is ready," announced Tanya's mother.

"Good timing," said Tanya. "With the good news about the fire, we can relax while we eat."

"Thanks be to God," said Mrs. Brandt.

* * *

At first Tanya and Eric mostly ate rather than talked. Finally, as they began to fill up, the talk increased. Eric related his evacuation experiences. He talked about living out in the wilderness. Tanya told about the publishing of Eric's book.

Then Eric cleared his throat. Looking at Mrs. Brandt and then at Mr. Brandt, Eric began to speak. "Tanya and I have something special to talk to you about. We have known each other quite awhile. There was some misunderstanding that pushed us apart for awhile, but that is all straightened out now. I would like to ask you for your permission to marry your daughter."

Tanya's parents turned and nodded in silent assent. Then Mr. Brandt spoke. "I know that ordinarily a father would say he would want to get to know you better, Eric, before agreeing to an engagement—and I do want to get to know you better before the marriage. But I know Tanya has had other marriage proposals and turned them all down. She had a good head on her shoulders, she knows right from wrong, and we trust her judgment. We grant our permission, Eric."

"Eric," said Tanya's mother, "I welcome you as the son we never had."

"And, son, if your cabin owner decides to sell your cabin, it'll be our wedding gift for the two of you. You know, Eric, I've been in real estate all my adult life and heard about acreage values since I was a boy, and land is one of the best gifts a person can give."

"That's very generous of you, sir. The last I heard, the owner is leaning towards full-time in Florida."

"If you'd like, call me 'dad.' You can have one in Detroit and an extra one in Marquette."

"You can have an extra mom, too, if you wish," added Mrs. Brandt with a smile.

"That's great. A wife, two moms, and two dads. What more could a man want?"

"A cabin in the woods," said Mr. Brandt with a chuckle.

"That goes for what this *woman* wants, too, dad. I liked the camp as soon as I walked in the door last winter. It's like an extra home. I'll sure have lots of homes. Your home and summer cottage, my home and Eric's camp. And now I'll have an extra family downstate, too!"

There was a short pause from all the exciting news. Then Mrs. Brandt asked, "Would you like some coffee and cake?"

"Sure," said Tanya. "You know how I like to eat. So does Eric."

"Would you two like to spend the night?" offered Mrs. Brandt. "I know you don't have a home to go to yet, Eric. We have plenty of spare bedrooms."

Before Eric could answer, Tanya said, "I don't know about Eric, but I'd like to return home. If the wind changes, I'll have to evacuate for the fire, and I want to rescue my valuables." Tanya wanted to save her Bible with all the notes written in it, her Christian music books, photo albums, and camera. "If Eric would rather return to our city, he can stay at my house. I have extra bedrooms."

Eric agreed, "I'd prefer to be closer to home, too."

Tanya and Eric had their dessert and then told Tanya's parents it was time for them to leave, because they were tired. Neither of them had enough sleep the night before with all the confusing noises and early morning interruptions. Tanya knew her parents watched the late news on television every night, and she asked them to call her if an evacuation of her area was announced. She knew she'd probably be too tired to stay awake until eleven. Eric thanked Mrs. and Mr. Brandt and shook their hands as he walked out the door.

* * *

Tanya and Eric each drove their own vehicle, with Tanya leading the way. They swung through town and stopped a few minutes to get the latest news on the fire. Everything was still under control, and the firefighters were still keeping a close watch. Eric knew where Tanya lived, because she had pointed to her driveway as they passed it on Easter morning.

Eric enjoyed the woodsy lane leading into the house. A few months ago, he would have been surprised at the size of the house, when it came into sight, but now he knew Tanya's background, so the beautiful spacious home designed to fit in with the wooded lot was not a huge shock for him.

They parked their vehicles and walked up to the house. Tanya unlocked the door, and they went in. Eric looked around the kitchen. "I sure like your old screened cupboard."

"With you living near a big city, I thought you might prefer modern furniture, Eric."

"I have modern furniture, because it came with my furnished apartment, but I like the patina of old woods and the feeling of connections with the past that comes with antiques. I specialize in history, remember. I'm not so fond of delicate chair legs, but I like the sturdy old furniture. I see more in the living room. I like your choices."

"Thank you. I'm glad to hear that," said Tanya. Come on. I'll show you the rest of the house. You have your choice of spare bedrooms. Would you like to take a shower?"

"I haven't had a chance to clean up today. I think I will."

"I guess we'll both want to turn in early. I'd like to watch the fire update on the eleven o'clock news, but I'm really tired," said Tanya.

"I am, too. I'm ready to turn in early."

"Would you like some popcorn and watch TV a bit before bedtime?"

"Yes. I'll take the shower just before I turn in."

In a few minutes, Tanya had microwave popcorn ready, and Eric had poured two glasses of pop. They went into the living room to watch TV, but first they watched five deer grazing in the valley below the house. Eric put his arm around Tanya, and she leaned her head on his strong shoulder with a peace that satisfied both of them. When the deer moved out of sight, they sat on the brown wicker settee.

Tanya and Eric had both grown a lot in the Lord in the last few months. They no longer faced the sexual temptation they had when the fire of love raged in their hearts that wintry night when they were leaving Eric's cabin. They were better able to control the fires in their heart. They allowed the Holy Spirit to be a damper for their emotions.

Neither did their love smolder in the loneliness of the spring and summer separation. The raging forest fire was the poker that stirred up the embers of their smoldering love. Some good had come out of the fire after all. The fire of the love in their hearts was rekindled for the rest of their lives. The fire might not rage as it had in February, but it would burn brightly until their hearts beat their final beats.

When the popcorn bowl was empty, Tanya put her head on Eric's broad shoulder and snuggled close to him. They were not really interested in the television program, so Tanya turned off the TV with the remote control, and they sat and listened to the song of the whip-poor-will, a lullaby of nature to end their full day of happiness together.

Now and then, the song of the bird was interrupted with a fire or police siren, but soon the vehicle was gone by.

Tanya and Eric eventually became so tired, they could barely get energy to walk to their bedrooms. Eric postponed his shower until morning.

Chapter 10

In the morning, Eric took a shower while Tanya prepared a hearty breakfast of bacon, eggs, and oranges. When Eric came into the kitchen, she told him to choose some tea for them from the tiny top drawers of her screened cupboard, and he chose English breakfast tea.

Tanya had turned on the radio for the morning news, and they sat at the kitchen table overlooking the valley to eat while they listened to the news. The faint smell of smoke drifted in from the open window, reminding them of the danger that had just detoured from them and had still not totally disappeared.

The newscaster said that some of the evacuees were able to return to their homes and camps, but some were still staying at the football stadium. Some didn't know if their homes and camps had escaped the blaze.

Tanya and Eric wondered what they could do to help. They decided to gather some supplies and take them into town. Living six miles from town, Tanya kept her cupboards well-stocked.

They gathered food, pop, teabags, instant coffee, sugar, and powdered creamer. They collected the teakettle, pans, silverware, napkins, paper towels, paper cups and paper plates, toilet paper, the kitchen chairs, folding lawn chairs, blankets, and pillows. Eric emptied his car. They loaded up both of their vehicles and headed into town.

* * *

On Main Street, the Salvation Army and St. Vincent DePaul people had set up canteens for the firefighters. They were well-supplied and running smoothly. The streets were full of people exchanging bits of fire news and worries about the fire. The restaurants were full, so many people just wandered around aimlessly, filling in the waiting time.

Tanya and Eric headed to her store. As they sat in her storeroom in the back of the store, Eric mentioned how worried the people on the street looked. “I know how they feel. My cabin is out there. I don’t own it, but I didn’t want it destroyed. I’m thinking some of those people still don’t know if their camps or homes are safe. Some are probably worried about the firefighters and any campers that might be missing. People will be concerned about the forest animals and beautiful trees. Even the tiny water creatures in the creeks would die in hot water.”

Tanya jumped off her chair. “I have it! I have it!”

“What do you have?”

“An idea. Let’s set up the food here in the store, so people will have a place to gather and talk. We can offer a place for people to pray. They need to change their worries into prayer requests.”

“Great idea,” agreed Eric. “Let’s get started.”

* * *

First Tanya cleared some display tables while Eric quickly unloaded the supplies out of their two vehicles. With teamwork a lot got done fast.

Tanya had a kitchenette in her storeroom and a small bathroom. Soon the teakettles were whistling merrily. The empty display tables were filled with sandwich supplies, packets of instant soups, snack food, foam and paper cups, cans and bottles of pop, teabags, instant coffee, sugar, and creamer. Tanya set out some Bibles from the bookshelves and Eric set up the lawn chairs.

Tanya made a sign: WELCOME—SNACK AND TALK AND PRAY WHILE YOU WAIT FOR THE FIRE TO GO OUT. BATHROOM AVAILABLE. She taped the sign on the outside of the corner display window and propped the door open.

* * *

With all the restaurants and bathrooms jammed, it didn't take long for people to start coming in—many who had never entered the store before.

The chairs filled up. Those standing congregated and talked. Some stood and ate and drank at the improvised tables, but it soon became evident that many of the people needed assurance more than food. Most had eaten breakfast at their own homes and then come out to get the tidbits of news about the fire.

Tanya asked Eric to rearrange the unpacked stock boxes in the storeroom into a circle for prayer. When this was done, Tanya offered to lead the first prayer group while Eric manned the food tables. Eric propped open the door to the storeroom, and Tanya made the announcement.

At first the store suddenly became quiet with self-conscious silence, but then one elderly couple went to the storeroom, and Tanya followed them, showing them where to sit. Tanya asked for their special prayer requests and began to pray, pausing occasionally and asking if they wanted to join in the spoken prayer. Both the man and his wife did.

The example of these three people encouraged others, and soon the storeroom began to fill up. People were more concerned about their spiritual needs than their stomachs. Eric saw this and asked if anyone in the store wanted to start a prayer group in a corner. Soon all the corners were filled with praying people.

Tanya and Eric traded places. Eric wasn't used to praying out loud, but the other people in the group kept the prayer going once Eric began.

The first requests had been for personal needs—the people's own families and friends and camps. Then the people began to add the camps of others, the evacuated campers, the firefighters, and the wild animals into their prayer requests. Then the requests became more spiritually oriented. Someone prayed that the fire experience would bring people closer to God. Another prayed that the fire would show people how they needed to be saved before they died. Another one prayed that the fire would bring backsliders back to God. Some people gave their adoration of God in prayer—His wondrous power and control, even control of fires. Some thanked Him for the firefighters arriving from all over the Upper Peninsula. Others thanked Him for the workers at the canteens and prayed for strength for the workers to keep serving.

As people became stiff from standing or sitting or kneeling in prayer, they wandered off to the food tables and bathroom. Some left to tend to their work responsibilities or return to their homes.

Other people came in. Prayer groups changed, but prayer continued all day. Frowns of worries disappeared, and the faces became calm with the peace of God.

Finally someone came in and announced the fire was almost out. Many people got up and left immediately, but some stayed to thank and praise God.

By early evening, the shop was empty. The floor was full of crumbs, and the grocery bags were overflowing with used paper towels and drinking cups and plates. Two people had accepted Christ as their Savior, and one backslider had returned to God.

Tanya and Eric were exhausted, but happy. Though they were usually neat people, they decided to leave the cleanup go until the next day. Eric took two of the kitchen chairs, Tanya turned out the lights and locked the door, and, with unspoken agreement, they took Eric's car back to Tanya's house.

* * *

Eric would not be able to return to his cabin yet, but he knew from the fire updates that all the camps in his area had been spared. He would be staying at Tanya's home again, at least for one more night, until the all-clear was given to return to his area.

Eric drove in the driveway and turned off the engine of his car. He got out, opened the door for Tanya, and took the kitchen chairs out of the back seat.

Eric carried the chairs into the kitchen. He and Tanya were too tired to even talk. Eric gently brushed Tanya's lips with his as he left her at her bedroom door before going to the spare bedroom.

Chapter 11

Tanya and Eric spent the next morning cleaning the shop. Quite a few people stopped in to thank them for their hospitality. Some people bought Bibles and other items; several were people who had never shopped there before.

By now the shop was back in order. Some of the merchandise was stained with drips of coffee, tea, and pop, along with smears of potato chip grease, but that was the least of Tanya's concerns. God would take care of the bookshop. God would take care of even the fire damage that had left a much wider strip of destruction than the guests at the bookstore had done. Tanya knew this for a fact, because she knew God's promise in Joel 2:25; "And I will restore to you the years that the locust hath eaten, the cankerworm, and the caterpiller…" The darkened badly-charred trees would stand as souvenirs of the fire, but the birds and animals would return, the grass would pop up a fresh green, and even some of the burnt trees would recover and drop seeds for more trees to sprout. The poplars would probably be the first new trees to appear. Any destroyed camps would probably be rebuilt. The woodland would again be a sanctuary for animals and people alike.

* * *

It was another busy, busy day, but by mid-afternoon, the shop was neat and clean and quiet, except for the soft music of the Christian radio station.

By late afternoon, word came through that evacuees were allowed to return to their camps and homes, except for the few that were burned out and could not yet walk on the hot ground. The Superior Dome emptied out. Most of the firefighters from the neighboring cities could return to their own towns, leaving the local city and township and Department of Natural Resources firefighters to keep watch and to continue wetting down the hot spots and dousing the small remaining fires with water. They would work in shifts and take turns getting sleep until everything was cool again.

Five o'clock arrived fast, and Tanya and Eric decided to go out to his cabin. They loaded the chairs, blankets, pillows, cookware, and leftover food and supplies into their two vehicles and went out to Tanya's where they unloaded everything and put it away. Tanya boiled some eggs, made a few tuna sandwiches, and took a few cans of pop and loaded them into a small cooler. Eric loaded his belongings into Tanya's Explorer. He would spend one more night at Tanya's to let the air clear of the pungent smell of smoke, and then move back to his home in the woods.

* * *

Driving all the way to Eric's camp together in Tanya's Explorer was a new experience for both of them. Now that the wedding and likely camp purchase were coming up, they knew they would be making this trip together many times in their lifetime, but none would be as thrilling as this first excursion.

Tanya hadn't been all the way to the cabin since her first and only trip there in February, and that was on skis.

Eric turned off Red Road, crossed a little creek, drove through some forest, and came out in the plains that gave view to the series of high bluffs in the distance. After going through the open plains and a stand of jack pines, the forest became a mixed growth of evergreens and hardwoods.

As Eric drove up the steep rocky hill to his camp and parked in the small clearing near his outhouse, everything seemed new to Tanya, seeing it for the first time without a covering of snow.

It all seemed different to Eric, too, because now he was seeing his surroundings with the enthusiasm of Tanya's joyful way.

Tanya wanted to look inside the camp again first. Then they walked the land, following the trail along the creek. The acrid smell of smoke was still in the air, but there was no smoke visible. They paused at a bend in the creek, overhung with tall cedars. It was a peaceful place to recover from the last few days of excitement.

They ate their supper at Eric's tiny rustic table, reminiscing about their memories of Eric's gourmet canned corned beef dinner.

* * *

After supper they sat on the sofa and rested awhile, quietly gazing at the rock cliff outside the windows.

Tanya said, "Maybe the camp will be full of noisy children some day. Maybe there will be a little Carlson baby added to the church pew by next summer."

Pointing his finger at Tanya, Eric teased her, saying, "Maybe we'd better get married first before these predictions!"

Tanya playfully swatted his hand. "You know we're planning to be married in a month. They'll be Carlson kids, not Brandt kids."

"If we have a boy, we could call him Eric Brandt Carlson."

"That would be nice," agreed Tanya. Then my last name can be part of our family, too."

* * *

When they both finally felt rested, they walked out on the porch and leaned over the rail to watch the rippling creek and listen to the tinkling sound of the tiny waterfall. They stood there, each quietly, privately, contemplating in a lazy sort of way.

Eric began to feel philosophical as well as lackadaisical. "Think of how this tiny Beaver Creek flows into the Dead River. Then the Dead River dumps into Lake Superior, and the water goes through the banks of the St. Mary's River and Soo Locks and into the other Great Lakes to the St. Lawrence Seaway and into the Atlantic Ocean which borders Europe, Africa, and South America as well as North America. How interconnected things are."

Laughing, Tanya said, "Even someone from the Upper Peninsula of Michigan can get related, by marriage to someone from Southern Michigan. That's an amazing connection, too!"

They laughed together, hugged, kissed, and then held hands as they walked back into the camp to repack the ice chest, lock up, and drive back to Tanya's, completing the circle from Tanya's to Eric's and back to Tanya's again. Soon it would simply be the Carlson circle—Tanya and Eric would become one at the church altar, joined for life.

Book List of Mary Goloversic

(Some books already printed; others printed soon.)

NOVELS

Iron Heart—historical novel set in an iron mining town in Upper Michigan in 1905-1928; story of love and heartbreak, hard work and fun, kindness and cruel social lines that make it almost impossible to cross from Miners' Hill to High Hill (possibly followed by three sequels: *Iron Wall*, *Iron Shaft*, *Iron Gate*)

Living on the Edge—story of a young woman growing up on the edge of town in the 1950's and facing an unplanned pregnancy

Raging Fire—exciting novel set in the wilderness of Upper Michigan in current times

Diary of a Drunk—fictional approach to the life of a drinker with Scriptures to combat the lies leading to drunkenness; appendix includes a section of "Discover the Truths" and materials to set up a D & R Club (Discover and Recover)

Games of a Gambler—fictional approach to the life of a gambler from a child through adulthood, with Scriptures to combat the lies leading to gambling; appendix includes extensive information on many of the lies of gambling and materials to set up a GG Club (Gambling Games)

AUTOBIOGRAPHIES/BIOGRAPHIES

I Married a Troll—true story of the humorous and serious side of the thirty-five (plus) years of the marriage of the author and her husband

Joys of Raising Boys—true story of parenting the three sons of the author and her husband

DEVOTIONALS

Imprints for your Mind—a collection of three short Christian living books, something for everybody; includes: *Minutes for Men*—related to men's work, remodeling homes, cars, sports; *Scents for Women*—related to housework, careers, hobbies, cooking, fashions; *Sounds for Teens*—about school, driving, athletics, social life, fun, music

Photos for your Eyes—a collection of devotionals illustrated with drawings and photos and backed up with Scriptures; includes: *Reflections of God in Nature*, a book describing the ecology of the Upper Peninsula (U.P.) of Michigan; *If Houses Could Talk*, a life history of a house and its inhabitants, told from the perspective of a talking house; *Towers, Turrets, and Tombstones*, a book related to architecture and tombstone art; *The Headless Bride*, a short short story about loving your spouse unconditionally; *Birth of a Book*, the story of the author's writing books for God

Diary of a Yooper—a collection of daily insights of the author.

CHILDREN'S BOOK: **Raining Cats and Dogs and Fish**—a collection of seven illustrated pet tales for ages 2 to 102, (children and the young at heart of all ages), all backed up by Scriptures; includes: *Wheel Gang*—a group of ocean creatures learns how love is better than cruelty, prejudice, and isolation; *Capture Camera*—a boy learns to be content by seeing what can happen when a person keeps wanting more and more; *Sarah the Siamese Cat*—true story about being kind, even if others aren't kind (author's cat); *Candy the One-eared Cat*—a book about accepting people as they are, including people with disabilities and deformities; *Crandon the Curious Cat*—a cat learns how curiosity and experimenting with sin can lead to danger, drunkenness, drugs, and being behind bars; *Mischievous Mopsy*—a funny, true story about a friendly, smart, but selfish greedy puppy (the author's dog); *Adventures of Boo Boy*—story about a dog that disobeys and runs away from home (the author's husband's dog)

SUCCESS SYSTEM—series of books containing strategies and Scriptures to become the person God wants you to be. The series includes books for adults, teens, and children. The books include original graphics, songs, and other extras. Everything is backed up by the Bible. The first five books cover 182 everyday living topics and teach people how to be a success.

The eight steps to success are:

1. Read Truth in the Bible, 2. Recognize lie in your life, 3. Repent of sin related to lie, 4. Replace bad thoughts, words, and actions with good ones, 5. Love, 6. Forgive,

7. Communicate, 8. Help (Each step involves God, others and you). Though you can't change others, you can change yourself, and others can learn from the changes in you. The success book includes ways to recognize lies and discover and apply truths leading to salvation and godly success; they are written in a timesaving sentence outline style; each topic is an entity of itself, so a person can zero on any topic in any order to meet any current interest of any immediate need.

Books #1-7 are designed for adults and teens.

Books #8-10 are designed for children, but can be used by adults and teens.

1. **Travel to Success**—topics cover the 8-step plan for success, problem-solving, counseling, finding truths, recognizing lies, regretting wrongs, restoration of losses, patience with your progress, replacements for bad habits

2. **Successful Love**—topics include God's love, people-pleasing, self-acceptance, health, cigarette smoking, alcohol and other drugs, neglect, abuse, suicide, marriage, hormonal problems, sexual relations, abortion

3. **Successful Forgiveness**—topics include salvation, sinning, confession, choosing a church, forgiving yourself and others, revenge, grudges

4. **Successful Communication**—topics cover lies, worry, memories, fear, gossip, complaining, criticizing, prejudice, blame, discouragement, anger, speaking out

5. **Successful Help**—topics on rebellion, feminism, machoismo, occult, greed, materialism, gambling, finances, perfectionism, procrastination, priorities, scheduling, helping others, being used by users, responsibilities, role models

6. **Success Memo**—condensed information from topic box of each of 182 topics, including_Scriptures

7. **Success Club Manual**—materials for any teen or adult to set up a Success Club for the group study of the success books; each meeting includes a topic from one of the success books, prayer, encouragement, and practical application of the Scripture to daily life situations; the manual includes a leader's guide, member's handbook, songbook of success songs, invitations to meetings, diplomas, plans for graduation and group parties, and much more

8. **Stubby the Stubborn Kitten**—a humorous children's book for ages 2-12 (actually can be read and enjoyed by people of any age); illustrated with actual photos of a cat called "Stubby" (owned by the author); covers 30 topics about everyday living in God's way; the 8 steps to success are brought out

within the thirty topics; includes Scriptures quotes for God's truths and teaches how to recognize lies; reader's guide with questions at the end of the book

9. **Stub Memo**—a daily memorandum of the thirty topics in the "Stubby" book, including Scriptures

10. **Stub Club Manual**—manual includes everything needed to set up and conduct Stub Club meetings for children (as well as for teens and adults); includes music, games, meeting guide, and other materials to help stub out sin and go forward to success for God

About the Author

MARY GOLOVERSIC (author of 18 books)

When I was nearing fifty, a three-month experience at a Skid Row mission in Chicago became a turning point in my life. Someone told me that I was believing the lies of Satan from the pit of hell, and then the person showed me how to sort out lies and truths. I began to think—if I, a person who was active in church and was teaching a ladies' Bible study, got deceived by lies, then many other people were also being deceived. I realized that we are not only deceived by the devil, but by other people, by some advertisements and some media, AND by ourselves with our own deceptive thoughts. We are all deceived, but we are all deceivers, too. I began to share this life-changing information with others to guide them to success in all aspects of their lives. Before I realized it, I'd become a writer, so I could share this information worldwide.

My writings center around the many forms of love—its meaning, its expressions, its use and misuse. In fact, "love" is in the middle of my long last name, "Goloversic"

When we learn to give and receive love in a godly unselfish way, present hatred will dwindle, past hurts will heal, and future hurts will be prevented.

Though I never planned to become a writer, all my life I was preparing for it, not realizing how I would use the knowledge and wisdom. Of course, my two college degrees with majors in education and numerous minors in many areas, were useful for writing—the research methods, literature, history, biology. Decades in the teaching field helped me develop techniques for getting my ideas across to people of all ages.

Years of studying piano and art for enjoyment enabled me to write songs for the books I write and do the illustrations and photos. Attendance at church services and Bible studies (in person and tuning into Christian radio programs) and extensive Christian counseling guided me to discover Bible truths to battle the lies life brings each of us. Eventually I used these Scripture references to back up my written statements in my books.

My pastimes of people-watching, taking nature walks, plus traveling throughout the U.S.A, Canada, Mexico and living two years in Spain, provided pictures in my mind that I could turn into words on paper.

Marriage and parenting three sons gave me insight into family living. My friends show me the lasting value of true friendship. I probably got part of my imaginativeness from my mom.

My tender heart gave me sympathy, but accidents, illnesses, surgeries, and troubles of all sorts gave me empathy. If I hadn't had all these heartbreaking experiences, I would not have become the storyteller that I now am.

My sense of humor adds a bit of frosting to the cake of my writing career.

Without my faith in God, I would have accomplished little, but He gives me the strength to complete the many books; and, through His promises, I have confidence to keep going. He gave me my talents, and I use them to serve Him.

www.ingramcontent.com/pod-product-compliance
Ingram Content Group UK Ltd.
Pitfield, Milton Keynes, MK11 3LW, UK
UKHW041821200726
13854UKWH00001BA/257

9 780759 683051

Matthew Burden's excellent research demonstrates connections between two historic movements in hymnody and missiology, encouraging us to further consider the impact of corporate worship songs on the life of the church.

David Clem, PhD
Dean of the Greatbatch School of Music, Houghton University

Matthew Burden eloquently makes the point that the global mission movement was birthed and is sustained in the midst of believers' worship. It is especially humbling to note that Baptists and Congregationalists were at the forefront of the mission movement during a time when a global mission focus and the conversion of the "heathen" was not a well-accepted priority for the church. This unique lens of viewing mission through the lyrics and the tunes of worship at the time will intrigue your mind, warm your heart, and bless your soul.

Rev. Sharon T. Koh, DMin
Executive Director/CEO, International Ministries
(formerly known as American Baptist Foreign Mission Society)

Burden presents compelling evidence that the hymn revolution captured not only the imagination of God's people but led them to rediscover the biblical call to global missions in a way that changed the world forever.

Matthew Smith
Singer-songwriter, Indelible Grace

Let the Earth Rejoice: How a Revolution in Worship Launched a Global Mission Movement provides fascinating insight into the previously unexamined impact of music on the "modern missionary movement." Matthew Burden carefully researches how mission-themed hymns entered the worship of seventeenth- and eighteenth-century Nonconformist congregations and convincingly traces their influence on early mission advocates such as William Carey. This book is thoroughly researched, exemplifies scriptural teaching that mission flows from worship, and raises thought-provoking questions about the nature and influence of music in contemporary Christian worship.

Rev. Reid S. Trulson, DMin
Executive Director/CEO Emeritus,
American Baptist International Ministries